To the readers who make this all possible.

*I wrote this novella for myself because I wanted to know what happened
between Daciana and Elias in Andorra Sector. This standalone
novella is a glimpse into my creative process when I allow the voices to
dictate the rules. I hope you enjoy their story.*

"THEY NEVER CAUGHT ME," SHE WHISPERED, gazing up at me through thick, blonde lashes. "Until me."

"Until you," she agreed, arching into me. "My cycle begins soon. On the next full moon."

"I know." It was another difference between Ash Wolves and X-Clan Wolves. Our Omegas went through estrus at their own intervals. But not Daciana. She would go into heat every month for several days at a time.

And without an Alpha to satisfy her cravings, it would hurt. I couldn't even imagine what she went through while hiding every month to avoid her pack.

No wonder she withstood all that pain in the lab. This female was emboldened by her past, hardened by her necessary choices. A strong Omega. My perfect mate.

"Will you help me through it?" she asked softly. "Or shall I run and hide once more?"

"You could try," I replied, leaning down to run my nose along her jaw, drawing my lips up to her ear. "But I would chase you again. Find you. And fuck you until you begged me to stop."

She shuddered, her damp center coating my cock in a fresh wave of slick.

Mmm, it seemed she liked the thought of that.

The pulse of my knot indicated that I did, too.

"I don't know if I could ever tell you to stop," she murmured, grabbing on to my shoulders. "Just don't growl. Please."

My tongue circled her thrumming pulse, reveling in the steady, quick beat humming beneath her skin. When I claimed her, I would bite her here. And her slight tremble confirmed she knew it, too.

"No growling," I repeated, acknowledging her limit out loud. "Any other requests, Daciana?"

"No sharing." The words were so quiet I almost missed them.

"Never," I said, dragging my teeth along her throat before lifting my head to capture her gaze with my own. "I would never share you."

X-CLAN SERIES

ANDORRA SECTOR

X-CLAN: THE EXPERIMENT

X-CLAN
The Experiment

USA TODAY BESTSELLING AUTHOR
LEXI C. FOSS

X-Clan: The Experiment

Editing by: Outthink Editing, LLC

Cover Design: Jay R. Villalobos with Covers by Juan

Published by: Ninja Newt Publishing, LLC

Print Edition

ISBN: 978-1-950694-44-0

X-CLAN
THE EXPERIMENT

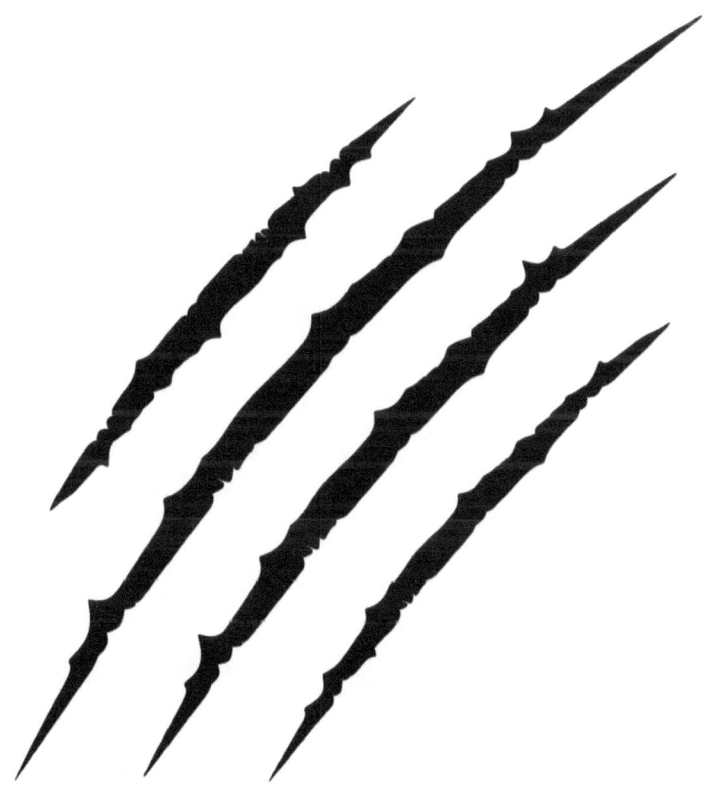

ABOUT X-CLAN: THE EXPERIMENT

Daciana

I'm an offering. A test. A pawn in an agreement I know little about.

Fly to Andorra Sector.
Allow them to experiment.
Mate an X-Clan Wolf Alpha.
Hope for the best.

Those are my orders. My fate. My current existence. There's nowhere to run, and the moon is a clock I can't ignore. One of these Alphas will claim me, assuming our genetics are a match. And if not, well, that's a fate worse than death.

Tick tock.
Make a choice.
Your future depends on it.

Elias

The pretty little blonde wolf has seen too much pain for her young years.

It makes me want to fix her.
To adore her.
To show her there can be good in this world.
But our future is wrapped up in an experiment.

Either she's compatible or she's not. The moon will determine our fate, or perhaps my inner wolf will decide it for us. Because with each passing moment, it becomes harder not to claim the female who I know in my heart is very much mine.

Run, run, little one.
And don't look back.
For if I catch you,
I just may bite.

Note: This is a standalone novella featuring characters from *Andorra Sector*, Book One of the X-Clan Series. It has Omegaverse elements and features a happily-ever-after ending.

PROLOGUE

DACIANA

Dear Human,

Here's what you need to know: The Alphas make the rules and the Omegas obey. So do the Betas, but this story isn't about them. It's about me and how I ended up in a sector far away from my homeland.

The Sector Alphas want to test my ability to mate, to determine the true worth of an Ash Wolf Omega to an X-Clan Wolf Alpha.

One of them will force their knot on me, which is really just a glorified way of saying he'll fuck me for days on end to

ENSURE I'M FULL OF HIS SEED. AND I'LL ACCEPT IT BECAUSE THERE ISN'T ANOTHER CHOICE.

I'M TOLD THIS WORLD IS DARKER THAN THE OLD ONE, PRIOR TO THE INFECTION THAT KILLED NINETY PERCENT OF THE HUMAN POPULATION. NOT THAT I KNOW MUCH ABOUT IT. I'M A SHIFTER OF THE CURRENT TIME, NOT THE FORMER ONE. AND POWER EXCHANGE IN MY CLAN IS VERY REAL. I KNOW HOW TO SUBMIT. I KNOW NOT TO FIGHT. AND I ALSO KNOW HOW TO RUN.

WILL I ESCAPE MY FATE? OR WILL I RUN HEADFIRST INTO IT?

THE FUTURE REMAINS UNCLEAR.

WELCOME TO ANDORRA SECTOR, WHERE THE WOLVES ARE MORE DANGEROUS THAN THE INFECTED LURKING OUTSIDE THE GLASS WALLS. ALTHOUGH, BOTH SPECIES DO HAVE ONE THING IN COMMON—THEY BOTH LIKE TO BITE.

WISH ME LUCK,
DACIANA

CHAPTER ONE

DACIANA

I COULDN'T STOP SHAKING. Everything felt wrong. This place. The scent. The *males*.

Oh God… The Alphas here wanted to eat me alive. Their need stirred an ache deep inside me that I fought with every fiber of my being. Reacting to them in any way would be seen as an invitation. And that wouldn't end well for me.

"Give me your arm," the physician demanded.

I complied because I always complied. Omegas submitted. Alphas ruled. Betas just existed.

If only I'd been born a Beta. A thought I'd considered countless times. Not that I could do anything about my status.

The needle pierced my vein, another blood sample

being drawn. At least they weren't playing between my legs today. *That* was an uncomfortable exam. The petite blue-haired Omega who'd managed that part of my exam had apologized countless times. I'd remained mute even though I desperately wanted to know how an Omega had obtained such a position in an X-Clan Sector. The rumors surrounding X-Clan Wolves were vast, mostly about how Omegas held no status in their society other than to be treated as glorified pets.

I knew that going in. Understood my fate. Accepted it, even.

If my body was found compatible, I'd be used by an Alpha male. Claimed. Possessed. Impregnated. And kept.

Not my first choice for my existence, but I was born without rights. A commodity to be traded. And the Shadowlands Sector Alpha had done exactly that— traded me to Andorra Sector to be tested, fucked, and eventually owned.

A shiver traversed my spine, my vision hazing beneath the harsh overhead lighting.

They kept taking blood.

Samples.

Poking.

Prodding.

Telling me *nothing* while keeping me tied to this damn chair. Oh, they claimed I wasn't a prisoner, that they only strapped me down to ensure I didn't move during the procedures, but I knew better. If I tried to flee, they'd catch me.

Hence my Alpha babysitter.

He stood silently beside the door, hands tucked into his jeans, observing. His fathomless dark gaze gave nothing away. *Elias*, the Sector Alpha had called him. Power oozed from him, denoting him as a high-ranking official, perhaps even the second-in-command.

I didn't know for sure because he hadn't spoken a word to me.

But he occasionally purred.

Just a subtle little rumble, typically appearing when my anxiety reached a high point and continuing until he finished calming me down.

He only touched me when he had to lead me somewhere. Never a comforting caress or a seductive pet. Merely practical and protective.

"Ceres," he said now, his voice deep and sensual. "I think you've tortured the girl enough for one day."

"I still have four more tests, E." The Beta physician tapped his needle, getting ready to stick me again.

But the Alpha's growl stopped him. "I said, you've tortured her enough for one day."

I swallowed, his aggression serving as an aphrodisiac to my senses. My next heat cycle was fast approaching with the coming full moon. It was part of the reason Dušan sent me when he did.

A test.

To see if an X-Clan Alpha might mate me.

God, it would hurt. I'd very likely pass out from the pain. And he'd continue to rut me, regardless of my fear and torment.

Alphas only cared about one thing—procreating.

Well, and telling everyone what to do.

That part just came naturally to them.

A bitter taste entered my mouth as the two males stared each other down. It didn't take long for the Beta doctor to concede, Elias clearly the more dominant of the two.

"Fine," Ceres snapped, setting his medical devices down. "I want her back bright and early to make up for lost time."

"She'll return when she's ready to return," Elias replied, pushing off the wall. "You've practically drained her anyway. What more could you possibly take?"

"You're a commander, Elias. I don't tell you how to do your job, so try not to tell me how to do mine, yeah?" Ceres left the room without waiting for a reply, the door slamming on his way out.

Elias arched a dark brow at the exit and blew out a breath. "Prick," he muttered before focusing on me.

I hadn't moved because I couldn't. Ceres had strapped me to the table, only leaving my arms free. While I could technically unbuckle myself, I didn't dare try it.

Elias approached, his focus on my bands. "May I?" he asked, briefly meeting my gaze.

My forehead crinkled. *Did he really just ask permission to touch me?* No. No way. He must have meant that rhetorically.

But when I didn't reply, he looked at me again, this time with a hint of irritation in his gaze. "Do you prefer to lie here all night, then?"

"N-no," I stammered.

"No, don't remove the straps? Or no, you don't want to stay here all night?" He really was a handsome male. I particularly liked the way the light played off the coffee-colored pieces of his otherwise dark brown hair.

What would he look like as a wolf? I wondered, idly distracted. *Strong. Dark fur. Midnight eyes.*

"Daciana," he snapped, drawing my focus back to him with a shudder.

"O-oh. Remove. Please." I swallowed. "Sorry." I closed my eyes, wincing at how pathetic I sounded. Alphas always intimidated me. This one even more so because of the energy rolling off of him.

Strong.

Virile.
Male.
Available.

My inner wolf preened in response, liking him as a potential mate. But he would never choose little old me. I wasn't an X-Clan Wolf, just an Ash Wolf Omega. A stand-in alternative for those who needed mates. A male like this one would wait until he found a proper female. One who was like him. Not an experiment stuck in a lab.

Besides, *I* didn't want *him* either. Or any male, for that matter.

A total lie, of course.

But I repeated the mantra daily, reminding myself that I didn't need a mate to have worth. Who cared that none of the Ash Wolf Alphas had taken a liking to me? That my own Sector Alpha decided I was more valuable to him as a commodity rather than as a female in his lands?

Yeah, I cared.

I cared a lot.

Elias's hot palm cupped my cheek, causing my eyes to fly open. He stared down at me with a compassionate gaze. "I'm not going to hurt you, Omega. No one is. Okay?"

I didn't know how to reply to that. Because just his scent told me how untrue that was. Alphas enjoyed fucking Omegas. He might never choose me as a mate, but if I went into heat tomorrow, he'd be the first one inside me. Just to knot. To procreate. To spread his seed.

That made him an obvious threat.

All Alphas were.

They took. They never gave.

His brows came down. "You're terrified of me."

I considered that. No. Terror wasn't right. Fearful, yes. But not of him, necessarily. Just of what I knew he could do.

7

An Alpha in a rut had the potential to inflict immense pain, even while providing pleasure.

That was what I feared.

His thumb traced my trembling lips, his expression still unreadable. "What did Dušan tell you before sending you here?"

It wasn't Dušan who had spoken to me, but his people. They'd mentioned that the parameters of the agreement included mandatory courtship, but I knew better.

Then that weasel Caspian had confirmed my suspicions on the plane ride here.

I could still hear him cackling in my thoughts, joking about how the hungry X-Clan Alphas would probably tear me apart with their cocks. It was rumored that this sector hadn't seen an unmated Omega in over five decades.

Yet the Alpha I met yesterday had smelled like one. Ander Cain also hadn't shown an inkling of interest in me, which I suspected was due to my Ash—

"Daciana," Elias said, drawing my focus to him once more. "This silent game of yours is unsettling my wolf."

I swallowed, noting the truth of his words in his gaze. I lifted my hand to his face, my thumb tracing the dark circles beneath his midnight eyes. "You need to go for a run," I whispered, sensing his wolf's longing for the shift. That was the aggression I felt from him. Not his yearning to take me, but the animal lurking inside, dying for freedom.

Mmm, he reminded me a bit of Dušan and the way his wolf always seemed to pace beneath the surface.

Of course, I didn't really know Dušan, only having seen him from afar.

He was the Alpha of Shadowlands Sector and far too busy for an Omega like me.

Too tiny.

Too blonde.

Too meek.

A pawn in a game of chess, one he'd traded for a shipment of items I knew nothing about.

So much for Omegas being the revered ones of our race.

My own kind didn't want me. Probably because they thought I was broken after everything that'd been done to my mother.

Am I broken? I wondered. *Maybe.*

I released the Alpha and stared over his shoulder at the ceiling.

Only, he moved to fill my vision once more. "What about you?" he asked softly. "Do you need to go for a run?"

Did I? I shrugged. "Won't make much difference what I want, will it?" I mused, feeling bold. It would surely backfire, but what did I care? I literally had nothing to lose.

These males would take my body.

Force me to mate.

And turn me into a glorified breeder, should my uterus prove to be a hospitable host.

The band around my middle unsnapped with a jolt that had me hissing on an exhale. The fabric had been cutting into my skin, decreasing my circulation, and the sudden increased flow to the region created a sting in its wake.

Elias frowned at me, then grabbed my gown to whip it upward.

Everything inside me went cold.

Maybe I misunderstood the threat of his wolf. This male intended to take me now, here on this—

"Jesus Christ," he breathed, his palm a brand against

my exposed belly.

A tear fell from my eye, my legs still bound and in an open position, thereby revealing everything below the waist.

It would only be seconds now.

He'd position himself and—

My hospital gown fell, and I was met with a pair of furious eyes. "Why the hell didn't you say something?" he demanded.

I frowned at him. "Wh-what?"

"You're all bruised." He quickly unfastened my legs, then walked around to start searching through the drawers. "Fuck. I don't even know what I'm looking for." He popped his head out the door and yelled, "Riley! Get your ass in here!" Then he started pacing and shooting angry looks my way.

I nearly curled into a ball, but just flinching hurt my sides, so I remained absolutely still on the table.

"You did not just command me to get my ass in a patient room," a feminine voice said from the hallway before the physician from yesterday stormed into the room.

"Don't even start with me," he growled in response. "Ander might be putting up with your feisty shit right now, but I will bend you over my knee and smack that fine ass of yours. Hard. And send you home whining to Jonas."

The Omega physician narrowed her eyes at him, hands on her hips, squaring off in the doorway. "Jonas would kick your fucking ass."

"And it'd be so worth it, just to hear you cry out," he returned, crowding her.

She slammed a bold palm against his chest, causing me to cringe. This would not end well. How did the Omega not know proper etiquette with Alpha males?

They preferred bowing. Submission. Placating. Not arguing.

"Get your testosterone-filled Alpha bullshit away from me, Elias," the audacious female said, her tone brooking no argument. "Now tell me why the hell I'm in this room."

He growled low in his throat. "You're lucky you're useful."

She blew him a kiss. "You love me and you know it."

"Yeah, yeah." He ran his fingers through those unruly dark curls, shaking his head. "Jonas needs to discipline you more."

"Don't I know it," the female replied, a smile in her voice.

What the hell just happened? He was allowing her to get away with this behavior?

"Impossible Omega," he muttered, refocusing on me and going into Alpha aggression mode once more.

Oh, damn. It seemed I would bear the brunt of her disobedience. Just my luck.

I nearly bolted into the corner as he flew at me to whip up my gown again. However, the palm against my throat held me in place.

Only, it wasn't a harsh hold but a tender one.

Like he was trying to offer a hint of security while showing my body to the physician.

I frowned beneath the fabric of my patient gown, wondering why he would do such a thing.

"Shit," Riley said.

I flinched on a hiss as she prodded my side.

"Why the hell did Ceres tie her down so tightly?" Riley snapped.

"I don't know, but I'll be asking the Beta that as soon as I see him again."

Riley snorted. "You mean you're going to punch him

in the face and then ask him."

"The method of questioning is still being determined," he admitted darkly, drawing the fabric down again with the hand not holding my neck. "Can you give her something to help with the pain?"

"Yeah, I'll be right back." She left the room and I swallowed, his palm still on my throat.

He stroked my pulse and gazed down at me. "Next time, say something."

"Like what?"

"That you're in pain," he said, his teeth clenching over each word.

I frowned. "I've been in pain since I arrived. Am I to complain each time he jabs me with a needle? Each time he pulls blood from my already depleted veins? Each time someone sticks a wand into my privates?" I huffed a broken laugh. "Pretty sure you don't wish for me to complain all day long, Alpha."

CHAPTER TWO

ELIAS

My blood boiled.

This infuriating little Omega had been in pain the entire time and hadn't said a word.

The restraints were meant to hold her in place while Ceres worked, not to keep her tied down out of fear of potential escape. She had nowhere to run. We all knew that. Except maybe the girl on the table because she clearly feared me. Feared *us*. Feared life.

And I wanted to kill whoever ingrained such a reaction into this beautiful little creature.

Riley returned before I could reply, a little cup of pills and a bottle of water in her hand. "Take these," she instructed the Omega before meeting my gaze. "Can you pour her a bath later? Add some healing salts? It'll help her relax a little."

I nodded. "Yes."

Her lips twitched, gratitude showing in her blue eyes—the same color as her hair this month. Riley always dyed her hair. But we all knew she was a natural redhead because her fur never changed with her mane.

She left saying to wait a few more minutes while she prepared the supplies, and I focused on the docile female on the table. Aside from taking the pills and swallowing them, she hadn't moved. Almost as if she feared being reprimanded for even breathing without permission. "Do you want to stand?" I asked her softly.

She frowned at me. "Do you want me to stand?"

"I want you to be comfortable."

Her light-colored eyebrows rose to her ash-blonde hairline. "Comfortable? In a medical lab? Tied to a table?" She seemed to consider her words, her brow furrowing once more. "Is that even possible?"

While I didn't care for her tone or her words, I was happy to hear her speak because it proved she wasn't yet broken. I'd worried about her mental state during these last twenty-four hours, what with her timid behavior and silent games. But she seemed all right beneath the docile exterior.

Well, all right enough, anyway.

The whole hiding-her-discomfort thing had to stop.

Granted, she had a point. Nothing about this situation was comfortable.

"You're taking tomorrow off," I decided just as Riley returned. She must have heard my comment, because her forehead scrunched in surprise as she set a bag of bath materials down on the counter. "You and Ceres have enough samples for now. I'm going to show Daciana around the sector tomorrow. And we're going for a run in the mountains. It's not up for debate. Ander will clear it."

Because I'd make him. He might be the Sector Alpha, but he was also my best friend. If I told him the girl needed this, he'd listen.

"Yes, sir," Riley said with a mock salute.

"You seriously want me to whip your ass, don't you?" Fucking naughty little vixen. "I'll never understand how Jonas handles you."

"Does he handle me, or do I handle him?" she asked, pretending to ponder.

"Oh, I definitely handle you, little brat," Jonas said, appearing in the doorway. "Stop torturing Elias."

"I've done no such thing."

"Your mate is full of shit," I informed him.

"I'm aware," the big man replied, narrowing his gaze at his female. "You're setting a bad example for our guest."

"Or maybe I'm setting the right one," she countered with a saucy grin.

Jonas growled, low and meaningful, prowling forward to snatch the back of her neck. "Let's go."

Riley giggled as the Alpha threw her over his shoulder and smacked her hard on the ass.

I shook my head after them. The man was a saint who fucking loved his mate.

"Will he beat her badly?" Daciana asked, then covered her mouth as if she hadn't meant to mutter the words out loud.

"Beat her?" I repeated.

"I'm sorry. I didn't mean—"

"Oh, I think I know exactly what you meant, little one." I leaned over her, purposely invading her space because I wanted to read her through scent. "He'll likely spank her for being a brat, but she'll enjoy it. Because that's their game. She often acts out for attention, and he punishes her in kind. Then they fuck and she comes all over his cock, and falls even more in love with him."

Daciana's cheeks turned bright pink, her breath hitching in her throat as the subtle aroma of slick permeated the air.

Mmm, yes.

Those words registered just fine.

"We don't beat our mates in this sector," I told her. "And unless I've completely read Dušan wrong, I don't think they do in yours, either. So who led you to believe these lies?"

She started to squirm, indicating I'd struck a nerve. Well, that was too bad. I wanted to know who the hell filled her head with this shit.

"Don't go silent on me now, princess," I drawled. "Tell me who painted your expectations so bleakly."

"Is now when I complain about pain?" she countered softly. "Or shall I remain mute once more?"

Her words surprised me, causing me to rear back. "I'm not even touching you."

"Not all pain is physical, Alpha," she said softly, her pale blue eyes drifting to the wall. "Sometimes it's our memories that torment us."

A powerful statement that told me so much. "Your mother suffered abuse from her mate."

"My mother didn't have a mate," she whispered. "She was a Beta, used by Alphas without mates of their own."

Oh, fuck… I ran my fingers through my hair. Because I knew what she meant. Some Betas made a profession of servicing Alphas. I'd visited several in my years. But they weren't built like Omegas, their bodies not as accustomed to receiving an Alpha male's brand of fucking.

Which meant most of them ended up hurt.

"All Alphas are the same and only want one thing," Daciana continued. "Yet none of them touched me, even when I offered to take her place. Because they didn't want to knot or to claim a mate. No, the Alphas of my home only wanted to dominate and destroy." She shook her head, seemingly lost to the thoughts in her mind. "She died, you know. That's why Dušan sent me. I had no one to leave behind."

"He actually said that?"

"He didn't have to," she said softly.

"That doesn't sound like the Alpha I've met," I admitted. While I knew the Alpha to be a hard-ass negotiator, he clearly had a soft spot for his Omegas. Why else would he add the courting requirement with the trade deal? None of the Andorra Sector Alphas could mate the Ash Wolf Omegas unless the female agreed. It wasn't how we typically did things as X-Clan Wolves, but that didn't make it wrong. Actually, if anything, it seemed rather right.

"I've never met him," she replied. "Too far up in the chain of command, and I was just a whore's daughter."

I frowned at her. "You shouldn't speak about your mother like that."

"Why not? It's what everyone else called her." A tear left her eye, one she either didn't notice or didn't feel fit to brush away. "They didn't even bury her afterward, leaving me to do the task after they finished rutting." She shook her head as if to knock the recollection away. "I'm sorry. It's not appropriate to discuss these things. I know better. I can accept whatever punishment you feel I deserve."

I gaped at her, the words, *What the hell happened to you?* flirting with my tongue.

But I knew what had happened to her.

She'd been the daughter of a Beta whore.

We had several here in Andorra Sector—something the vast Alpha male population required—but Ander ensured they were all taken care of properly with health benefits and adequate pay and care.

It had me questioning what the hell Dušan's camp was up to over in Shadowlands Sector.

I brushed the tear from her cheek and drew my fingers down her neck. "Can you walk, Daciana?"

She'd endured a lot of tests today and still hadn't made any effort to move from the exam bed.

"Yes," she replied, pushing upward with shaky movements.

I watched as she stood, saw the way her knees wobbled with uncertainty. "You need to eat," I realized out loud. "And Riley wants you to take a bath."

Daciana merely nodded, her gaze on the ground.

She still thought I meant to punish her.

What world did this poor Omega grow up in?

While she bathed, I would find out—by calling Dušan directly. "Come on," I said, lifting her up into my arms as her wobble turned into a violent tremble. While she could walk, I suspected it would hurt. She was too weak from all the blood loss, and that bruise around her middle clearly pained her more than she was letting on.

I cradled her carefully and walked over to the table. "Can you grab that bag for me, princess?"

She reached for it, then held on to it as if it were the most important job of her existence.

Taking her back to her sterile quarters seemed cruel, so I headed to the elevator to bring her to mine. My bathtub would be bigger. My view was also nicer, as my windows overlooked the city rather than a drab courtyard, and I preferred the idea of sleeping in my bed tonight instead of on the couch in the side room.

Ander probably wouldn't like it.

And the buzz against my wrist confirmed that notion as soon as I stepped off the elevator onto my floor. I didn't look at the message, knowing what it would say, and instead focused on Daciana's comfort. She watched me warily as I set her in an oversized chair in my living area. "I'm going to grab you a tray of snacks and some water. After I'm satisfied with how much you've eaten, I'll pour you a bath."

Then I'd deal with my Sector Alpha and the Alpha of Shadowlands Sector.

Daciana fell back into her silent routine while I fed her. But at least she ate without complaint. I just wished I could get rid of that distrusting glimmer in her gaze.

I tried talking to her, telling her a little about my family and the days before the Infected caused chaos in the world. How I grew up in Spain but studied up in Norway, which was where I met Ander. I continued into the background of Andorra Sector, how Ander became the Sector Alpha, why we preferred technology and healthcare research, and she listened with a placid look. Not necessarily disinterested, but not exactly intrigued either.

So afterward, I poured her a bath and carried her into the marble interior of my bathroom. "I added the salts as directed," I said, gesturing to the bag Riley had prepared. "Let me know if it's too hot or too cold." I'd tested it myself, but my body temperature tended to run a bit on the warm side.

She stared at me for a long moment, then turned to the bath and stepped inside—with her gown on.

I caught her elbow and she flinched, her eyes squeezing shut.

"Jesus, if I wanted to hurt you, I would have already," I said, slightly irritated by her constant fear of my nearness. "But you can't wear that thing in the bath. You need to take it off."

She swallowed, a tear leaking from her eye.

"What is it you think I'm going to do to you?" I demanded, cupping her cheek with my free hand and using my opposite to grab her hip and turn her toward me. "I'm trying to take care of you, Daciana."

19

"Wh-why?" she asked, trembling. "Wh-why are you taking care of me?"

"Because it's the decent thing to do?" I suggested. "Because you're a guest in our sector." I slid my thumb under her chin, tilting her head up and encouraging her to raise her eyes to mine. "Because I'm not a complete dick."

Her light blue irises swirled with an emotion that she squashed almost as soon as it appeared. One that suspiciously looked a lot like hope.

Dropping her hands to the hem of her patient gown, she began to lift it up. I released her as she tugged the garment over her head. She tossed it to the side, leaving her naked before me.

I held her gaze, proving a point, and offered her my palm. "Lower yourself slowly. I want to make sure it's not too hot."

She glanced down at my hand, then closed her eyes and accepted my help. The way her body shook told me how weak she felt.

"No more tests," I said more to myself than to her. "Not until you feel better, anyway."

Daciana went back to her preferred silence, but I caught the way her shoulders relaxed as she settled into the water. There was no wincing or any indication of pain, her hand loose in mine, not tense. If anything, she appeared soothed as she laid her head back on the towels I'd rolled into a makeshift pillow.

"I'll be back to check on you in thirty minutes," I said, releasing her.

"Thank you," she whispered, warming my heart a little.

I leaned over to kiss the top of her head. "You're welcome, princess."

She sighed, the first hint of comfort coming from her

tonight. With a nod to myself, I left her to soak and quickly pulled up Ander's messages on my phone.

What the fuck are you doing?

Stop ignoring me.

I will come up there, Elias.

Fucking answer me, you dick.

I smirked.

The last one arrived four minutes ago. *You have five minutes.*

I walked to my front door and opened it to wait for his arrival. And the elevator dinged right on cue.

He stormed into the hallway and paused upon finding me leaning against the wall just inside my condo. His eyes narrowed in suspicion. "Why do I feel like this is a trap?"

"It's not. But I do need you to call Dušan for me."

He frowned. "Why?"

"Because he sent us a broken Omega and I want to know why."

CHAPTER THREE

DACIANA

I FROZE UNDER THE WATER, my blood running cold at the scent of a second Alpha.

Ander Cain, I recognized, my stomach knotting.

This had all been a setup. A way to relax me before whatever punishment Elias had in mind. I shouldn't have spoken so freely, knew better than to say those things, but something about him made me want to loosen my tongue.

And now I would pay the ultimate price.

They'd put me in a tub, readied my body, and would take me harshly. Force me to enjoy it. Use their growls to provoke my pleasure.

Tears threatened to fall, but I swallowed them.

I had to be strong. It was the only way to survive.

Although, some days, I wondered what the point of living in this world was when fate clearly had it out for me.

A growl came from the other room that had my hair standing on end.

Then deep murmurs followed.

My ears twitched as I picked up the conversation with my wolf hearing.

"What do you mean, 'broken'?" Ander demanded.

"She had to bury her mother, Ander," Elias told him. "After a pack of Alphas rutted the poor Beta to death."

I flinched at the crude description, then remembered how I'd told him pretty much the same thing. It was hard to sugarcoat such a horrendous experience.

"Fuck," the Sector Alpha muttered.

"Yeah. *Fuck.* I want to know what kind of operation Dušan is running over there that could ever allow this to happen."

Oh, no… This wasn't good. He couldn't talk to Dušan. Not about this. If he found out I'd mentioned this, he'd… he'd… well, I didn't know what he'd do, but it couldn't be good.

Grabbing the sides of the tub, I tried to pull myself up, but my limbs were too heavy.

No, no, no. I couldn't let my lethargy stop me. I had to—

"Dušan." Ander's voice came out clipped and I froze yet again.

"Cain," a deep tone returned.

Oh, shit. He'd already called him.

I sat motionless, listening, dread pooling in my belly. Interrupting them now wouldn't suit. And what would I even say? Stop? I nearly laughed, even as a sob threatened to break free.

Omegas had no power.

They'd never listen to me.

Besides, I had earned whatever punishment was coming my way because I knew better.

I never should have said anything.

"Why are you calling me unannounced?" Dušan demanded. "Is there a problem with the Omega?"

"I'm going to let Elias answer that," Ander replied.

I held my breath, needing to hear his response even as I feared it.

"Daciana seems to think I'm going to beat her, Dušan. No, not just beat her. She's under the impression that I'm going to rut her to death. Like your Alphas did to her mother."

Silence.

Followed by a grumbled curse from Dušan. Or I assumed it was him because it hadn't come from Ander or Elias.

"Ionut, one of my *former* Alphas, was running a prostitution ring near the edge of my territory. It came to my attention about two months ago. I destroyed it and all the Alphas involved four weeks ago. Daciana was one of the victims taken into protective custody. Upon discovering she was an Omega, I designated her for Andorra Sector, wishing to provide her with a fresh start. I had no idea she was this... shattered."

I flinched at the word.

Is that what I am? I wondered. *Shattered?*

"She mentioned burying her mother," Elias said quietly.

"Yes." Dušan cleared his throat. "It happened shortly before the raid. It's a death on my conscience, as it could have been avoided had we intervened earlier. I don't have an excuse."

"Because a good Alpha never makes excuses for a failure," Ander said quietly. "I understand."

More silence.

"Do you wish to return her in exchange for another?" Dušan asked calmly. "We can make arrangements as needed."

"That won't be necessary," Elias replied. "She might be broken, but we have the means to put her back together."

"You're certain?" Dušan pressed.

"We'll discuss it and get back to you," Ander cut in. "Thank you for the details, Dušan."

"Of course."

A tense silence followed and I suspected the call had ended.

"You're sure you want to shoulder this burden?" Ander asked what felt like hours later. Either I'd missed some part of the conversation or the Alphas were staring each other down and communicating with their eyes.

"I can help her," Elias said softly. "I *want* to help her."

"The details described are the breeding grounds for a lifetime of struggle. She won't trust you easily."

"I know."

"And you'll have to be patient."

"Yes, I know."

"You're not a patient man, Elias."

"I can be patient for her," he stressed, a note of pleading in his tone that caused my lips to curl down. Was he really begging his Alpha to let me stay? Why?

Another tense stillness followed without sound.

Then a deep sigh. "All right. If she's your chosen, I'll do what is needed to back you up. But you better court her, E. It's part of the agreement."

"I'd never force her," Elias promised.

"I know." A clap followed—Ander smacking Elias on the back, maybe? "You're a good man when you want to be."

"Wow, thanks, man. What a compliment."

"I try," Ander replied, a grin in his voice. "Let me know how things progress, and I'll meet with Ceres about the test results."

"Oh, that reminds me," Elias said. "Ask Riley about the belts today and how tightly that asshole strapped Daciana to the table. Her abdomen is one giant fucking bruise."

"*What?*" the Sector Alpha roared, causing me to cringe.

All this aggression was doing things to me, conflicting my morals.

When my heat cycle hit during the full moon, I was in for a world of pain.

"Yeah, so you can understand why I won't be allowing him to run any more tests on her likely ever," Elias said, surprising me.

Likely ever?

"Fuck."

"That's your favorite word of the night," Elias murmured.

"It's the word that describes my life right now," Ander muttered, sounding tired.

"That wouldn't have anything to do with the stubborn little Omega you have locked up in your condo, would it?"

The Andorra Sector Alpha sighed. "I have no idea what to do with her."

"Mate her," Elias said. "That's what you need to do with her. She's already pregnant with your child. Finish the job."

"She hasn't learned her lesson yet."

Elias laughed. "You know what? I think you both deserve each other. A match made in Stubbornville."

"Don't ever change your profession, E. Comedy isn't

in your genes."

The distinct sound of a fist meeting flesh reached my ears, shocking me from my bath.

Then male grunts followed.

More of that dominant energy filled the air, causing my thighs to clench as slick threatened to spill.

Alphas fighting. Oh God. No. I couldn't handle the violent fallout. Didn't want to be the one they expelled that aggression into when they finished.

Because I knew that was my future.

They would grapple, draw blood, then focus that attention on me and knot me from both ends. It would hurt even while I came, my body built for betrayal.

I would hate being an Omega in that moment. Would crave death even while I screamed their names.

A laugh broke through my thoughts.

The sound of a thud following.

Then another chuckle as Elias wheezed, "I give. I give."

"I know," Ander replied, his tone triumphant as a scuffle of shoes over carpet hit my ears. "You almost had me, though."

"I did," Elias agreed. "But you sucker punched me."

"Shouldn't have given me your side."

"Yeah, yeah," Elias grunted. "You want a drink?"

"Nah, I need to get back to my Omega, and I'm guessing you need to see to yours."

I frowned.

That sounded... *homey*.

"Mmm, my Omega," Elias murmured. "Yeah. I think I like that."

He couldn't be referring to me, right? Maybe Elias had another somewhere?

No. No, he couldn't because there were no available Omegas in this sector. Well, except the one I'd scented yesterday. But she seemed to belong to Ander, if I'd followed their conversation right.

Maybe there were more?

Had Andorra Sector lied to Dušan about their need?

Well, even if the sector did have another Omega, I hadn't scented one on Elias. And he hadn't left my side since we met. However, he could have one hidden away somewhere, I supposed.

Although, her scent would be in this condo, and all I smelled was him. This was definitely *his* den.

If he had an Omega, there'd be a lingering trace of her somewhere.

But he couldn't possibly mean me. I wasn't his Omega. Nor should he want me. I was just the shattered Ash Wolf.

"You don't appear very relaxed," a deep voice said, causing me to jump in the water.

Elias stood in the bathroom, leaning against the door, watching me.

I hadn't heard him approach, or the other Alpha leave, too lost in my thoughts to pay attention. A very dangerous place to be.

"More silent games?" he mused, stepping closer to crouch beside the bathtub. "What if I tell you I like your voice? Will that provide you with the courage to speak?"

I blinked at him. "Speaking to you creates trouble."

His eyebrows rose. "Oh yeah? What kind of trouble?"

I opened my mouth to comment on his call to Dušan, when it struck me that no punishment had been demanded as a result.

Actually, Dušan had sounded almost contrite and apologetic. Not angry at me for speaking. I tilted my head, considering. "Why didn't he care that I told you?" I wondered out loud. "I spoke out of turn. He should demand a whipping."

Elias's eyes widened, then a hint of understanding crossed his features as he rested his forearms on the bathtub. "You listened to our conversation in the other room."

Another infraction, I realized, wincing. I was just screwing this up left and right. Yet I couldn't bring myself to apologize. I should. I knew I should. But I couldn't—*wouldn't*—say the words.

"I'm glad you told me, Daciana," Elias admitted quietly. "It helps me understand your reactions." He dipped his hand into the water near the edge of the tub and frowned. "The water is cold."

"Yes," I agreed.

He gave me an irritated look. "I told you to tell me if you're uncomfortable."

"I'm not uncomfortable," I replied, frowning at him. "I grew up taking baths in water much cooler than this."

He stood and walked to a cabinet, pulling out a plush towel. "Stand up, Daciana."

I swallowed and grabbed the edges of the tub again to try to adhere to his command. My fingers slipped, the lip of the tub rather large for my smaller hands.

A hand appeared before my eyes. I traced the limb up to his face, finding him watching me intently. Not in a hungry way. No, he appeared more concerned. "Daciana," he murmured, flexing his fingers.

I pressed my palm to his and allowed him to assist me upward. He lifted me effortlessly out of the tub and helped me find my footing on a plush mat before wrapping me up in the world's softest towel. I marveled at how the fabric felt against my skin, burrowing into it on instinct and longing for a nest of such high quality.

Elias watched with that keen expression, then went to his cabinet and pulled out several more towels before leading me to a bed bigger than my room back in

Shadowlands Sector. "You can sleep here," he said, setting the towels on one of the pillows. "Feel free to make yourself at home."

My lips parted because I understood what he was saying.

He'd just invited me to nest.

Something he confirmed as he walked to another closet to pull out a pile of sheets and blankets, which he placed on the nightstand.

"I'll find you something to wear," he said, returning to the bathroom and walking through it to another room beyond. When he returned with an oversized shirt that smelled like him, I began to understand that he'd invited me to nest not only in his condo but in his very bedroom.

I studied him. "Do you intend to sleep here, too?" It was a fair question, given this was his room.

"Only if you want me to, princess." He stroked his knuckles over my cheek. "If not, I have a guest room down the hall that I can rest in."

"Why not give me the guest room?"

He stepped closer and cupped the side of my neck. "Because my intent is to eventually share this bed with you, but not until you're comfortable."

"You wish to knot me?" I whispered, swallowing thickly.

"I wish to do more than knot you, Daciana." He moved closer, his thighs brushing mine as his palm slid to my nape. "I intend to mate you, Daciana of Shadowlands Sector."

"But we don't even know if I'm compatible yet," I sputtered. "A-and I'm not… You're not… I mean… This isn't…"

"Shh," he hushed, brushing his lips over mine in the gentlest of kisses. "We have time to figure this out, Daciana."

No, we don't, I wanted to tell him. He had to know my heat cycle was about to start. All female Ash Wolves went into estrus during the full moon.

"I'll never force you into anything you're not ready for," he continued. "But I'm an honest male, and part of that means telling you the truth about my intentions. So yes, I want you to nest in my bed. And yes, I hope to one day join you. However, you will dictate our pace, not me."

He pressed his mouth to mine once more, lingering just a breath longer before releasing me. I felt cold in the wake of his absence, my body longing for more of his heat, his caress, his kiss.

The arrogant curl of his lips told me he knew my thoughts as plain as if I'd spoken them aloud, but wouldn't give me more until I asked. "I'll be in the living area for a few hours if you need me. Try to get some sleep and we'll go for a run tomorrow."

He left me standing beside his bed, gaping at the door.

He's courting me. He's really and truly courting me.

Hearing the males discuss it had been one thing.

Having Elias actually do it was entirely another.

An Alpha wants to mate me.

How was that even possible?

No, better question: Did I want him to court me?

That… that I didn't know.

But even as I thought it, I heard my wolf whispering, *Yes. Yes, he's mine.*

31

CHAPTER FOUR

ELIAS

KNOCKING ON MY OWN DOOR FELT WEIRD, but I wanted to provide Daciana with a warning that I intended to enter. When I heard nothing on the other side, I pushed through and paused on the threshold at the sight on my bed.

A nest.

I tiptoed toward it, studying the structure and memorizing her patterns.

Beautiful, I thought, my breath leaving me on a reverent exhale.

I'd never actually seen a nest before. Omegas were rare in Andorra Sector. Hell, they were rare, period. Just more so here as we hadn't seen the birth of one in over five decades. Other sectors were luckier, their mating cycles more regular, while Andorra was filled with Alphas and Betas and only a handful of already claimed Omegas.

Hence the need for the trade with Shadowlands Sector.

If the Ash Wolves proved viable for procreation and mating, our problems would be solved. Well, mostly. There were still those who believed only an X-Clan Wolf would do, but I found myself growing less and less picky by the minute. Especially with the beautiful blonde female sleeping soundly in the middle of my bed.

She'd taken my invitation to nest seriously, surrounding herself in plush linens and swathing herself in one of the towels. Or perhaps that was the same one I'd wrapped around her after the bath.

And she'd used the shirt I'd provided as a pillow.

I smiled. Whether she realized it or not, she'd efficiently bathed herself in my scent. I rather liked that.

Her eyes slowly opened, revealing a pair of beautiful blue irises that gazed lazily up at me. She didn't frighten or cringe, just watched me as I watched her, both of us waiting for the other to make a move.

I wanted to take her running, to give her a tour of her new home. But finding her pliable and sweet like this gave birth to so many other ideas.

Such as sliding into her nest and holding her.

Kissing her soundly.

Fucking her in her little safe haven and leaving my scent behind for her to seek comfort in later.

I had lived nearly a hundred years, dying for a mate. Now that I finally had a viable candidate, I wanted to claim her as mine before anyone else could be given a chance. No one would fault me. Not even Ander. But Daciana's past required me to tread carefully. If I took her the way my wolf desired, she'd see me in the same light as the Alphas who destroyed her mother. And I refused to let that happen.

"Are you hungry?" I asked softly. "I made breakfast."

She stretched her arms over her head, sighing as her bare skin met the silk of my sheets. "I haven't slept like that in…" She trailed off, scrunching her nose and then sighing. "Well, a long time."

My lips curled. "Do you want to lie in your nest all day instead of going for a run?" I wouldn't fault her for it. She'd been through a rough, well, life, it seemed.

"No. I want to see your mountains." She sat up, the towel slipping down her breasts. Rather than tug it back up, she sighed, utterly relaxed. "You made eggs."

"I did."

Her little nose twitched. "And something savory."

"Bacon."

"Mmm." She rewarded me with a very small smile, the first one I'd seen from her since she arrived. "I like eggs."

"Me, too." I crouched down so our eyes were level rather than me hovering over her. "Do you want me to bring them to you here, or would you like to join me in the dining room?"

Her pale irises stared keenly into mine. Just when I feared she might fall into her silent habit once more, she murmured, "You're courting me."

"Yes." No point in hiding the obvious. All my cards were revealed last night anyway. Not that I'd meant for any of it to happen. But when Dušan had offered to take her back, I'd reacted instinctively, shoving away the possibility of a trade. I wanted to be the one to help her heal because my wolf had already decided she was mine. I didn't know when it happened or how; however, I knew better than to fight fate.

She fell into that contemplative state again,

scrutinizing me intently.

Then she nodded. "Okay." A simple word that seemed to imply so much more. Acceptance, most of all. But also a hint of relief. And maybe a touch of pleasure.

She crawled out of her nest, her petite form completely revealed. For the first time, I allowed myself to examine her slightly curved assets.

Daciana was a little thin for my taste, but that could be fixed with a few decent meals. She stood about a foot shorter than my six-foot-four frame. Her shoulders were slender. Her breasts just shy of full. Her hips all woman. Her intimate curls blonde just like her head. And her legs were shapely in a way that told me she enjoyed a healthy run.

I took a step forward after finishing my admiration and caught her gaze with my own. "You're a beautiful woman, Daciana," I told her, palming her cheek.

She didn't reply, her blue irises locked on mine.

So pensive.

It wasn't distrust I saw lurking in her eyes, but curiosity as she waited to see what I would do next.

I bent my head slowly, not wanting to frighten her, and pressed my lips to hers. I meant for it to be a quick tease, a taste of the future to come, but the second our mouths touched, my control wavered.

Threading my fingers through her hair, I pulled her closer, my tongue slipping inside to meet hers. She gave a surprised little yip and grabbed my arms for balance, then melted into me on the sweetest little sigh.

Oh, this female redefined the meaning of perfection.

She fit into me like a puzzle piece I hadn't realized was missing from the grand scheme of my life. And now that she'd latched on, I couldn't let her go.

I pressed a palm to her lower back, my other hand remaining in her hair to angle her head to better deepen our kiss.

A low growl blossomed inside me, not one meant to intimidate, but a sound of stark need.

It caused my female to freeze, even while her slick permeated the air. She wanted me, her body responding naturally to my call, yet the tension shooting up her spine gave me pause.

I forced my lips away from hers, my eyes searching her expression for a clue.

Abject terror stared back at me, her pupils so dilated I couldn't see the blue of her irises. I frowned, confused.

Her arousal painted the air, her body clearly accepting my advances.

But that horrified look in her eyes wasn't one of submission or enjoyment.

Had it been there this whole time? Had I misread her cues when she returned my kiss? Or had I frightened her with my growl?

"What is it?" I asked her softly. "What did I do to earn that look from you?" I gentled my hold, releasing her hair to palm her neck instead. "Talk to me, Daciana. I need to know what I did so I won't make the same mistake again."

She shuddered, her throat working soundlessly as a violent shiver forced its way through her. I lifted her into my arms and settled her back into her nest, trying to surround her with the safety she clearly craved.

"I'll bring your eggs to you," I said, pressing a kiss to her forehead. "But once you've calmed down, I expect an answer."

Because I couldn't help her if she wouldn't talk to me.

Leaving her cocooned in her sanctuary, I ventured into the kitchen to retrieve the now cold breakfast plates and carried them into the bedroom. She was sitting up, her eyes alert and less panic-stricken as I returned.

Setting the plates on the nightstand, I dragged over one of the chairs from my en suite seating area and positioned it beside the bed. Daciana watched each move, reminding me of the way a lamb might observe a stalking wolf. When I sat down and handed over her food, she accepted it and picked up the fork lying across her eggs.

We ate in silence, both engaged in that staring game she seemed to favor.

Analyzing.

Considering.

Waiting.

This time, she would be the one to break the silence. Not me.

And she must have realized that because once she finished every morsel from her plate, she cleared her throat and rewarded me with her full attention. "They growled when they took her. Made her want it even while she screamed for them to stop."

"Jesus," I breathed, my stomach churning with the breakfast I'd just devoured. "Fuck, Daciana." I had no idea what else to say.

Actually, no. That wasn't right.

The way she described it... "Were you there?" I asked, a newfound horror entering my thoughts. "Did they hurt you, too?"

She shook her head quickly, then nodded, then shook it again. "No. I mean, yes. I... I was nearby. But they never touched me."

"Why not?" I wondered out loud, then realized how that sounded. "Sorry, that came out wrong. I'm just not understanding, because you're an Omega." Why would they choose a Beta over her? Not that I *wanted* them to touch her. It just didn't make sense.

"These Alphas preferred pain." She swallowed,

closing her eyes. "Betas can't endure like… like I can."

"They forced their knots on her," I realized aloud, disgusted. There was a reason Alphas preferred Omegas, and it went beyond procreation. Their bodies were literally built to receive our brand of aggression.

And now it made sense.

"They kept you nearby to facilitate their rutting." Because being able to smell the Omega would allow them to pretty much trick their bodies into responding.

I'd been with my fair share of Betas, had used them to sate my more brutal needs, but never like that. And I *always* provided aftercare.

"It's a good thing Dušan killed those males," I added, my voice a low snarl. "Or I'd be on my way to Shadowlands Sector to introduce those assholes to a real Alpha." Because *fuck*. That type of treatment was so fucking wrong.

Had I killed a female during sex before? Yes. A human. After sharing her with Ander.

One time.

Never again.

Because neither of us could stomach the aftermath.

That was why I'd demanded Ceres turn our most recent mortal addition into a shifter. I'd intended to seduce her with Ander but needed her to be unbreakable first. Of course, she'd turned out to be part X-Clan Wolf already, and an Omega as well. So that plan dissolved almost immediately.

But the point was… "That's wrong." I shook my head, trying to clear it of the images rioting through my mind. "So fucking wrong. A mating growl is meant to seduce, not to be used as a means of rape."

"If that's true, then why does it make a female wet even when she doesn't wish to be aroused?" Daciana countered, that gaze of hers radiating an intelligence that only added to her attractiveness.

I took Daciana's plate, placed it on top of mine, and set both on the ground before moving to kneel on the bed. She lay down, her pulse spiking while she watched me in that steady manner she seemed to favor.

"Alphas are at the top of the hierarchy for a reason. We're stronger and faster, the literal apex predator of the world. It's in our nature to want to mate, to dominate, to claim. And so we've been given certain gifts that allow us to ensure our goals are met." I slid into her nest, caging her between my arms as I straddled her hips. "We can take what we want, when we want it."

She swallowed, her body utterly still beneath mine. "I know."

"Yes, you do," I agreed, canting my head. "But just because an Alpha can do something doesn't mean he should. The growl is meant to entice, and when used appropriately, it can lead to gratifying results for both parties involved." I leaned down to skim my nose across her cheek, to press my lips to her ear. "I could take you right now, here, in the safe haven of your nest. You'd enjoy it. Scream my name. Come all over my cock as I knotted you so deep that it would hurt to breathe."

A note of fear mingled with the sweet scent of her arousal, indicating a battle looming inside her as her body disagreed with the memories of her mind.

Her wolf wanted me.

Of that I had no doubt.

But her mind, well, that required more convincing.

"We both know how easy it would be to force your acceptance, little one," I whispered, licking the shell of her ear. "I can smell your interest even now. But I'm not going to fuck you yet, Daciana." I nuzzled her neck, then pulled back to look deep into her eyes. "Do you want to know why, baby?"

I brushed my lips over hers, holding her gaze the entire time, sensing her inability to speak beneath the onslaught of sensations I'd just awoken inside her.

She liked what I was doing, and part of her wanted me to take her by force, as it would give her a reason to hate me.

Sadly for her, I knew better. Because unlike the Alphas of her former acquaintance, I maintained absolute control over my urges. And I never used them to purposely hurt another wolf.

"I'm not going to fuck you, because it's the duty of an Alpha to respect his female. And I know you're not ready, even if your body says otherwise." I grazed my teeth across her lower lip, growling softly to emphasize my point. "You're right about growls provoking certain reactions—whether compliant or otherwise—which is why it's up to the Alpha to know the difference between consent and forced pleasure."

She quivered beneath me, her eyes rolling back into her head on a groan as her slick spilled between her thighs—both in response to my call and my touch.

I trailed my mouth across her jaw and back up to her ear. "Make no mistake, Omega. I will force your pleasure, but it will always be because you want me to. Not because I used a growl to dampen your thighs." I sealed my lips over her pulse, sucking lightly before releasing her. "Now let's go for a run. I think we both could use the physical release."

CHAPTER FIVE

DACIANA

MY LEGS SHOOK WITH EVERY STEP.

Not because of the snow covering my new boots or the way my jeans clung to my calves, or even the exertion it took to walk up this wintry path of the mountain.

No, my thighs shook because of Elias.

And his words.

The way his teeth had skimmed my pulse.

His dominance.

Heat.

Oh, the way his lips felt against my skin.

I closed my eyes, recalling every sensation all over again, and nearly moaning as the deep-seated ache inside grew tighter and even more restless.

He knew, too. It'd been the entire purpose of his little

show of dominance in the bedroom. He wanted to show me how easily he could take me, regardless of my mental consent. Just as he forced me to see how well he kept the urge under control.

Because there'd been no doubt that he desired me. The evidence of it had been an obvious bulge in his sweatpants as he caged me under his much larger body. But never once did he rub against me or seek gratification. It'd all been a demonstration of his prowess and his ability to maintain control.

And it had also proved he read my body language exceedingly well because the second I reacted to his growl, he'd stopped and demanded to know why I'd frozen. But rather than make me answer him immediately, he'd allowed me to eat.

The male was a walking conundrum.

I didn't understand him.

He didn't react the way an Alpha should.

Or maybe... maybe he was acting the way a real Alpha should, and the ones of my experience weren't true Alphas at all.

Because every male we passed on our way to this path had glanced at me with mild curiosity, but nothing more. No one tried to touch me. No one called me a runt. No one belittled my Omega heritage. No one said a single harsh word at all, just a greeting at best, before leaving us to our afternoon of exploration.

Elias had shown me the town square.

He'd explained the various streets, how they connected, which paths to take to leave the dome, and then went as far as to show me the protocols of exiting. Thus leading us to our current place on the mountainside, away from the protective glass that covered his sector.

"Do you have protective measures in place for the

Infected?" I asked as we moved.

"Not needed. They don't come up here."

"Why not?"

"Because we're immune to them," he replied. "They don't like the way we taste or how we react to their nearness, so they stay away. It's why a colony of humans live in the caves over there." He pointed toward the west.

"You allow humans to reside nearby?"

He lifted a shoulder. "Ander does. So long as they stay out of our way, we don't bother them. Although, they do make for good sport every once in a while."

"For fucking?"

He glanced at me, amusement bright in his gaze. "For one so afraid of mating an Alpha, you do seem rather focused on sex, princess."

I snorted. "You're an Alpha. All you ever think about is fucking."

"I'm a man, sweetheart. That fact drives my urges first and foremost." He stopped to take in our surroundings as he added, "And no. I don't use humans for fucking. They break too easily."

"You use Betas instead."

A muscle ticked in his jaw before he looked at me. "I've never knotted a Beta. But yes, I fuck Betas. Because we don't have any Omegas."

"Except me." And that other female I kept smelling.

"Except you." He blew out a breath and rubbed the back of his neck with his palm. "Fuck it. Yeah, I've done some shit to females I regret. But I've only ever killed one—a human—which is why I don't fuck them anymore. As for the females of my past, you met two of them on our walk up here. It's entirely consensual and I take care of them."

I met two of them? I almost asked who, but he took a menacing step forward, irritation pouring off him in

43

waves.

"I really hope that was enough information for you, princess, because I won't be addressing this topic again." He caught my chin, holding me sternly but not harshly. "I like rough sex, and yes, I favor pain with my pleasure. I'm an Alpha. I require submission. But I do not kill females for sport." His jaw clenched, causing me to frown.

"What else?" I asked, catching the note of indecision in his gaze. "What else do you want to tell me?"

He growled in reply, but it wasn't the sexual kind, just a low warning that I'd pushed him beyond some sort of comfort level.

"I recently ordered Ceres to turn a human into a wolf so I could fuck her. Something about her had sung to my Alpha instincts. Fascinatingly enough, she had Omega genetics in her. Now she's an X-Clan Omega." He released me. "Ander intends to claim her."

Ah, that was the female I kept scenting.

Interesting.

Elias waited, his expression hardening when I said nothing in reply. If he expected his admission to bother me, it didn't. I grew up around Alphas who did a hell of a lot worse to humans and otherwise.

What irked me more than his actions was the fact that he'd wanted the female enough to turn her into a wolf.

That bespoke a connection—one he'd intended to explore.

"What would have happened had Ander not claimed her?"

"He hasn't claimed her yet," he corrected. "But it's a moot point. She's already pregnant with his child."

"And if he hadn't?" I pressed.

"Are you asking if I would have courted her?" he returned, arching a brow.

I jutted out my chin, arching a brow of my own. "Would you have courted her?"

"I never had a chance to see if there was a connection there, so I don't know." He stepped closer, the heat of his body rolling over mine even through our clothes. "She doesn't call to me the way you do, if that's what you want to know."

"I'm not really sure what I want to know," I admitted, gazing up into his midnight eyes. His irises were so hypnotic, like pools of strength I longed to lose myself within. It both scared and enthralled me. "I don't think I've ever met anyone like you, Elias."

His lips curled just a fraction. "The feeling is absolutely mutual, princess." He cocked his head to the side. "Ready to go for a run?"

I took in the landscape, considering the endless field of snow and trees around us. "You're certain there are no Infected?" Ash Wolves weren't immune to the zombie-like creatures in the same way his kind were, so I had to be careful.

"Positive," he replied. "I wouldn't put you in danger like that, Daciana."

My focus returned to him, noting the sincerity in his gaze. "Okay." I was aching to free my inner animal, to experience the new terrain beneath my paws and roll in the mounds of fluffy snow surrounding us. So beautiful and different from my home.

Not to mention the scents.

Mmm.

Yes.

I pulled off my sweater, boots, and jeans—all items Elias had provided, claiming they were gifts from Doctor Riley. Folding the borrowed items with care, I turned to find Elias just as naked as me.

Oh.

45

Seeing a nude male wasn't new. Shifters waltzed around without clothes all the time.

However, seeing this male in nothing but flesh was… well, it was very new. Very new indeed.

Because, um, wow. Yep. *Gorgeous specimen* were two words that came to mind. All carved lines of solid muscle from head to toe, which was pretty typical for a shifter, but on him seemed more intense. More masculine. More alluring.

I stepped forward, my fingers itching to see if he was as hard as he looked. Tracing the ridges and valleys of his torso, I determined he was exceptionally firm, and hot, too.

Virile male, my wolf appraised. *My male.*

I pressed my nose into his chest, inhaling deeply and sighing at his now familiar scent—a woodsy spice that had helped lull me into the best sleep of my life.

He leaned down to sniff my hair, his lips brushing the top of my head.

My arms slid around his waist, pulling him closer, losing myself in his masculinity and strength. The urge to climb him, to lock my lips with his, hit me square in the abdomen, drawing a little whine from my lips.

His chest rumbled in response.

Not in a growl, but in that soothing purr of a sound I'd enjoyed in the lab. I rubbed my cheek against his pectoral muscle, just above his heart, longing to hear it again, and he gifted me with another soft vibration.

I relaxed into him, warm despite the cool earth beneath my bare feet.

He folded his arms around me, holding me tightly, his lips in my hair.

"Thank you," I breathed, nuzzling into him. "Thank you, Elias."

This time he remained silent, perhaps unsure of how

to reply. A small smile teased my lips at the idea that I'd rendered the Alpha speechless. I also rather liked the reaction I felt against my lower belly where the well-endowed part of him rested against me.

Hot.

Hard.

Alpha.

An inferno stirred inside me, slicking my thighs in response, but I didn't give in to the arousal. I wanted to run first. And even more than that, I desired to meet his inner wolf.

"Show me your fur," I whispered, releasing him. "I've never met an X-Clan Wolf."

"Just as I've never met an Ash Wolf, at least not in wolf form." He took a step back, giving me a knowing look. "I'll show you mine if you show me yours."

"Deal." I reached inside to stroke my inner wolf, calling her to the surface and smiling as she immediately took my cue.

Shifting always hurt in the best way, as if I were being reborn into my true form. I often preferred being a wolf, choosing to remain on all fours for days at a time. My mother used to call me a loner. Others teased me about my smaller size when compared to those in my village. But I was the only Omega. They were all Alphas and Betas, and clearly bigger as a result.

My wolf might be slightly shorter in stature, but it helped me run faster than almost everyone I knew. I could also fit into spaces they couldn't, allowing me to hide when I needed to.

Which was far more than I cared to admit. But I found sanctuary in my animal half, enjoying burrowing and lying in wait.

Patience was one of my greatest strengths, how I survived in a world of madness.

Many chose to use their teeth or fists. I chose my mind. I observed. I watched. I waited for the right time to react. And I wouldn't have it any other way.

With a sigh, I opened my eyes and shook out my ash-colored coat. Streaks of brown ran through different parts, as well as patches of white, giving me a lighter color that allowed me to blend into the woods with ease.

Although, here, I would certainly stand out against the snow. However, in the summer, I could hopefully hide near the tree trunks and the earth, like I did back home.

A nip to my back leg had me spinning around to face a giant black wolf with ebony eyes.

Holy crap.

Elias was huge.

And so incredibly handsome.

We walked around each other, sniffing and nuzzling and introducing ourselves all over again. His woodsy-spice scent remained, but his coat was softer than anything I'd ever felt, just as I imagined mine appeared a bit shaggy to him.

His head butted against mine on our third circle, the affection in that touch causing me to return the gesture. He rumbled, gifting me with another of those unique purrs. I leaned into him in response, seeking more of that glorified strength.

Our wolves seemed to fit together, his size dwarfing mine in the best way.

I pranced around him, excited, curious to see how fast he could run.

His ears perked up, sensing my challenge. The smolder in his gaze dared me to start the chase.

I knew what would happen if he caught me.

The Alpha in him would force me to submit.

And when we returned to our human state, he would

fuck me as a result.

Which was why he'd given me the choice to initiate the game, to ensure I understood the stakes.

I wasn't a virgin. But I wasn't experienced either.

My first heat cycle had been with a Beta male. He'd done nothing for me, his seed not even strong enough to impregnate my womb.

After him, I went through all my heat cycles alone in the woods where no one could find me or scent me. Each time had hurt more than anything else in my existence, my intense need to procreate always left unsatisfied. But I preferred it to bedding an unworthy male.

This male was not unworthy.

And something told me hiding in the woods of Andorra Sector wasn't going to work for my next heat cycle.

I had to choose.

That was my entire purpose for being here—to entice an Alpha male. To mate. To prove whether or not Ash Wolves and X-Clan Wolves could procreate.

Elias had made the decision to court me.

It was on me to accept the courtship.

Only two days in this male's company and I knew everything I needed to know about him. Most wolves took less time to ascertain the viability of a mating. And if I was honest with myself, I knew from the moment I met him that he was a viable candidate.

Strong, powerful Alpha. My wolf would be lucky to call him a mate based on those characteristics alone.

Yet it was the whole package I desired now.

His concern for my well-being.

His protective nature.

The way he stood patiently, awaiting my next move.

How he allowed me my moments of peace and

contemplation.

His gift of the nest.

He'd more than proven himself a worthy wolf. It was time for us to dance, to test the boundaries of our companionship in the oldest of ways.

Catch me if you can, Alpha, I told him with my eyes, then took off up the mountain at a dead sprint.

CHAPTER SIX

ELIAS

DACIANA WAS FUCKING MAGNIFICENT, her ash coloring unlike any I'd ever seen. I could stare at her for hours and never grow bored, but she had another activity in mind. She flew up the path at a speed that called to the predator inside me.

I trailed her with a wolfish grin, adoring the way her pads lightly brushed the earth with each gallop. She barely left an imprint in the snow, her steps that quick and efficient.

Whatever weakness had ailed her after the lab visit yesterday was long gone, thanks to a full night's rest and a healthy breakfast. It was one of the many benefits of being a shifter, but that didn't mean I'd let Ceres near her again. Her bruises were gone, and I intended to ensure no one ever touched or hurt her again.

The only blemishes I wanted on her skin were ones delivered in the heat of passion. Marks she would enjoy receiving.

No more labs.

No more experiments.

We'd do this the old-fashioned way instead.

She darted to the left, into the trees. I followed, leaping over logs and snow piles, chasing my future mate as she played in her new terrain. My senses remained alert, guarding her every step, ensuring there weren't any threats nearby. While it was rare for an Infected creature to make it this far into our lands, it did happen on random occasions. Although, the last one was over a year ago.

We had nothing to offer them here other than a small cave of a few dozen humans. But they protected themselves rather well, killing any Infected before they could reach our sector walls.

That didn't stop me from being careful now, though, especially knowing how susceptible Daciana could be to a bite.

Would our child be immune? I wondered, pursuing her down a slope that led to one of the mountain's many hidden alcoves. Whether she meant to or not, she was wandering along one of my usual trails and exploring with her nose.

Daciana bounded over a mound of thick snow, then took off into another sprint that showcased her agility and strength. It was almost as if she wanted to prove herself a worthy mate, allowing me a glimpse of what she could offer.

My wolf responded in kind, keeping pace with her as she continued to explore, while providing the security she needed to feel safe.

Her demeanor slowly began to shift from curious and playful to something else as we ran. She glanced back at me, noted my nearness, and took off again.

I followed.

She ran faster.

So I quickened my trot as well.

Until we were both running at a dead sprint again around the mountain, her legs carrying her at an incredible pace.

My nose twitched at the hint of excitement drifting off her. A subtle scent that triggered my instincts.

Oh.

She wanted me to catch her.

This was a mating test.

A way of seeing if my wolf could outmaneuver and dominate hers.

Challenge accepted, I thought at her. Not that she could hear me, but she'd understand soon enough.

Noting our surroundings, I quickly selected the perfect spot to take her down. I just had to herd her into the right place.

A nip to her heel earned me a high-pitched yip as she turned the way I desired. When she started to deviate, I nipped her again, which caused her to growl. Had I been in human form, I would have smiled. My soon-to-be mate had some obvious tells. Which was how I anticipated her reaction to my nibbling at her leg again.

She turned on a snarl, and I tackled her into the snowbank, rolling down the hill and directly into a little nook in the hillside. I pinned her with my mouth over her throat, my much larger body pressing hers into the soft earth.

Mine.

I settled on top of her, waiting for her next move, expecting her to squirm or try to fight.

She did neither of those things and instead started to shift back into human form.

I immediately released her neck, engaging my own transformation to keep from accidentally hurting her. My claws and teeth with her delicate skin were not a good combination.

My human form appeared before hers—an indication of my superior strength—but she wasn't far behind.

I ran my nose along her jaw, inhaling the fresh scent of pliable female. We were protected from the elements here, enclosed in a small cave lined with dirt and rock. It smelled like earth and home, pleasing my animal side greatly.

"You caught me," she breathed, her heart galloping in her chest. I could hear the quick pace of it, felt the vibrations as if they were my own.

"I did."

"That makes you a worthy mate, Elias of Andorra Sector."

I smiled down at her. "Why, thank you, Daciana of Shadowlands Sector."

She didn't return my amusement, just scrutinized me in that studious way of hers. This female was unlike any I'd ever met, her eyes rarely giving anything away. But I could smell her interest. Could feel the heat of it blossoming between us as well, her slick coating her thighs and enticing my masculine senses.

"No one has ever caught me before," she admitted in a whisper.

"Do you often run?" I asked, watching her intently.

"Always." She wrapped her legs around my hips, placing her slick center against my growing arousal. "During every moon cycle, I hide. Alone. Never claimed by an Alpha."

I swallowed, her supple form radiating her intrinsic

need. Running as my wolf always excited my nerves, leaving me high on life and ready to fuck.

And it seemed it did the same to her.

Even more so since I'd caught her.

She appeared almost intoxicated by it, drowning in her feverish need to be claimed by the male who bested her.

"You've never been knotted."

She shook her head. "No. My only experience is from my first heat, many, many moons ago. A Beta male friend. I hated it."

I drew my thumb across her cheek, balancing my upper body on my forearms placed on either side of her head. "He couldn't satisfy you."

Another shake of her head. "It was awful."

"And you didn't trust any of the other Alphas of your acquaintance not to hurt you," I added, my guess based on the history she'd detailed. "So you hid."

"Yes. My mother forced me to run during my cycle because she knew what they would do to me if I went into estrus near them. So, like a coward, I ran and hid and they never caught me."

"Not a coward," I said, ensuring she felt the truth of that in my tone. "You outmaneuvered the Alphas. That makes you intelligent and brave."

"My mother distracted them for me," she admitted softly. "Most times they required me to remain nearby, but she always found a way to help me flee around the full moon."

Fuck. I couldn't even begin to imagine what those distractions required. "Did they ever chase you?"

"If they did, they never caught me," she whispered, gazing up at me through thick, blonde lashes.

"Until me."

"Until you," she agreed, arching into me. "My cycle

begins soon. On the next full moon."

"I know." It was another difference between Ash Wolves and X-Clan Wolves. Our Omegas went through estrus at their own intervals. But not Daciana. She would go into heat every month for several days at a time.

And without an Alpha to satisfy her cravings, it would hurt. I couldn't even imagine what she went through while hiding every month to avoid her pack.

No wonder she withstood all that pain in the lab.

This female was emboldened by her past, hardened by her necessary choices.

A strong Omega.

My perfect mate.

"Will you help me through it?" she asked softly. "Or shall I run and hide once more?"

"You could try," I replied, leaning down to run my nose along her jaw, drawing my lips up to her ear. "But I would chase you again. Find you. And fuck you until you begged me to stop."

She shuddered, her damp center coating my cock in a fresh wave of slick.

Mmm, it seemed she liked the thought of that.

The pulse of my knot indicated that I did, too.

"I don't know if I could ever tell you to stop," she murmured, grabbing on to my shoulders. "Just don't growl. Please."

My tongue circled her thrumming pulse, reveling in the steady, quick beat humming beneath her skin. When I claimed her, I would bite her here. And her slight tremble confirmed she knew it, too.

"No growling," I repeated, acknowledging her limit out loud. "Any other requests, Daciana?"

"No sharing." The words were so quiet I almost missed them.

"Never," I said, dragging my teeth along her throat

before lifting my head to capture her gaze with my own. "I would never share you."

Her blue irises flickered with an emotion that she quickly hid behind a mask of courage. "Don't hurt me."

I cocked my head a little, considering. "No pain without pleasure," I offered instead.

She frowned. "There is never any pleasure in pain."

"On the contrary, sweetheart. Sometimes the best pleasure is underlined in pain." I demonstrated by tugging her bottom lip between my teeth—just sharp enough to make her wince—then laved the hurt with my tongue before dipping inside to indulge her in a hungry kiss.

A moan slipped from her mouth to mine, her nails digging into my upper arms as she undulated her hips below in clear welcome.

"We'll negotiate pain and pleasure as we go along." I spoke the words against her mouth before locking gazes with her again. "Anything else?"

She slowly rotated her head in the negative. "No. Nothing else."

"If that changes, tell me," I told her, meaning it. "This only works if we communicate."

Words I'd never said to any other woman, mostly because I never cared about the others I fucked. But Daciana was different. I wanted a future with her, while the others were all passing amusements meant to fulfill my animalistic urges. And they did, just as I'd taken care of theirs.

However, this moment right now went much deeper than a mere mating.

This was an introduction to the future.

A relationship meant to span time itself.

A bond between an Alpha and his Omega.

Daciana swallowed, her pupils flaring as she pressed

her heels into my ass. "I accept these terms." She pressed her weeping cunt against my shaft and released an impatient noise that went straight to my balls. "Fuck me, Alpha. Fuck me now."

This time I nipped her bottom lip in reprimand. "The only one issuing commands here is me."

"Then do your job."

"Oh, little Omega," I said, slipping purposefully through her damp heat to position the head of my cock at her entrance. "You'd better hold on tight, baby, because I'm about to introduce you to a whole new level of pleasure and pain."

CHAPTER SEVEN

DACIANA

I SCREAMED AS HE ENTERED ME, my body nowhere near used to accommodating a male of his size and girth. My nails bit into his skin, my legs tensing around his hips.

Why the hell did I ask for this? I wondered, dizzy. I knew it would hurt. I knew he would lose himself to the rut. I knew it… would… *oh*… I liked the way he kissed me. As if he cared. He had my face cradled between his palms, his mouth gently moving against mine as he engaged my tongue in a sensual dance that distracted me from the pain below.

I wasn't even sure when the screaming stopped and our kiss began.

But now I didn't want it to ever end.

He tasted like spice and man, his lips full and plump against mine. So sensuous. So delicious. So sigh-worthy.

I melted beneath him, my muscles relaxing.

And he began to move.

It struck me then that he hadn't moved since his initial entry, his cock lodged into my channel, stretching me and forcing me to accommodate him without painful thrusts.

Now he slid in and out almost hypnotically. Slowly. Each rock forward seemed to seat him deeper and deeper, causing my eyebrows to lift in surprise.

He wasn't all the way in the first time, I realized, my heart racing.

That meant he hadn't lost himself to the rut at all.

He was completely in control.

I marveled at the discovery as a fire began to ignite in my lower belly, one that burned hotter each time he flexed his hips. *More,* I thought, meeting his movement with one of my own.

"Ohhh," I moaned into his mouth, arching sharply into him as the bundle of nerves between my thighs shot a jolt up and down my spine. "Again." My head fell back against the ground, my lower body writhing with the need for more.

"You're a bossy little thing, aren't you?" he teased, slamming his cock inside me with a force that caused my teeth to chatter.

It should have hurt.

It didn't.

Because I couldn't feel anything beyond the burning ache twisting inside me.

I needed more.

His heat.

His strength.

His mouth.

I tangled my fingers in his hair and yanked him down to me, kissing him without fear of punishment or rejection. I took what I wanted, how I wanted it, and the amazing male above me allowed it.

My heels applied pressure to his ass, begging him to take me harder.

He did.

My nails dug into his scalp, demanding he fuck my mouth with his tongue, just like his cock pummeled me below.

He complied.

Everything I asked for, he gave. His pace increased to match my groans. He swiveled his pelvis against mine to hit me where I desired him most. And he grasped my hips to angle me in a way that set my blood on fire with every thrust.

It was perfection.

The most amazing coupling of my life.

Surpassing all my expectations.

Because he let me drive, despite my position on the bottom. I could feel it in the way he read my body, reacting to my wants and needs with skilled maneuvers of his own.

I had no idea what I was really doing. He had to know that. Yet he followed my lead while teaching me little movements at the same time.

Like how to receive him deeper with a slight tilt of my lower body.

How to kiss without a lot of oxygen.

How to pet and stroke and drive one another mad.

"Please," I begged him, requiring something I couldn't articulate. Every time he brushed my clit, I wanted to cry out. It wasn't enough. Not even the savage thrusts could push me over.

Maybe I had to be in heat to come.

I had never really tried outside of estrus.

The thought had a tear slipping from my eye. I felt tightly strung, on the edge of bursting, almost like I did when I went into my cycle without a male and no relief in sight.

It burned.

Ached.

Had me scratching my nails down his back in fury.

He nipped my jaw in reprimand. "Patience."

I nearly snarled at him in reply. Agony ripped through me, drawing more moisture behind my eyes, and I snapped out his name. It was a warning and a plea wrapped up in one.

"I'll take you there," he said, drawing his nose along my cheekbone. "And we'll fly together."

I didn't want to fly. I wanted to explode. To rid myself of this growing torment, to release the inferno building inside and curl into a ball of replete silence.

But it would never come.

I knew from experience, had lived through it so many times in a hiding place of my choosing. Only, now I had a male who could offer me solace, but he held back and I didn't understand why!

My mouth clamped down around the tendon of his neck, my teeth piercing his skin.

His chest rumbled in response, causing me to freeze.

Only, it hadn't been a growl.

Not quite.

More an angry sound mingling with pleasure.

A groan.

"I'm going to knot you so deep you're going to beg me to release you, but I won't," he said, his voice low and tempting. "Fuck, Daciana. You're gripping me so tightly. So perfectly." He slammed into me, causing us both to cry out.

Now the rut was taking him.

Forcing him into a pattern of violence.

Only... I liked it.

Each thrust hurt but also mounted the pressure building inside me, heating me from within.

I clutched him to me, my legs squeezing as I held on with all my strength, taking what he gave me and demanding more.

Hot.

Hard.

Mmm.

His blood was in my mouth from my bite, the essence spicy and masculine. I licked my lips, craving another taste, but I couldn't move, his power too much for me to fight. I welcomed it. Reveled in it. Adored every meeting of our hips.

I felt him growing.

Sensed the knot pulsating at the base of his shaft.

My walls tensed, massaging the part of him I longed to feel, urging him to release.

"*Fuck*," he groaned, the sound a breath against my ear, his lips caressing my neck.

This is it. He's going to—

His knot shot out of him, securing itself deep inside me and fracturing my thoughts as I fell headfirst into oblivion.

"Elias!" I screamed, my body convulsing beneath his as waves and waves of pleasure rocked me from head to toe.

He cursed in response, my name falling from his lips soon after as if a word of prayer.

"Oh, oh, oh," I kept saying, my reality replaced by something so exquisite and real that I couldn't think beyond the rapture assaulting my spirit.

It went on and on.

Sucking me under its spell and blacking out my vision.
Yes, yes.
This.
I never knew it could be like this!
Elias moved.
The world shifting.
I allowed it, uncaring, too lost in my ecstasy to focus. He kept me warm. Safe. His arms hard around my back.

Some part of that seemed strange since I'd been on the ground before with my shoulder blades touching the earth. I squinted my eyes open and found my head against Elias's chest, my legs spread across his waist as his cock continued to pulsate inside me.

"I never knew it could feel like this either," Elias whispered. "I mean, I *knew*, but nothing beats the real experience."

I frowned. "Was I thinking out loud?" *Wow, is that my voice?* It came out raspy, as if I were yelling a lot.

He chuckled, his fingers brushing through my hair. "Yeah, baby. But please continue. It's great for my ego."

I lifted my head, balancing my chin on his chest. "Somehow I doubt that."

A deep rumble met my reply—his version of a purr. My shoulders instantly relaxed, my entire body going limp against his. "I love that sound," I admitted.

"I know," he replied softly, his fingers still in my hair. "I like how it soothes you." His touch moved to my back, smoothing downward and upward, petting me while the convulsions still vibrated through us both. "Did I hurt you?"

"No," I said, not even needing to evaluate the question. If he had hurt me, that pleasure at the end made up for it. And I wouldn't change a thing about our experience. Well, except for one part. "You didn't bite me."

I'd been prepared for it. Expected it. Yet it never came.

"Mmm, I wanted to," he admitted, his palm stilling on the center of my back. His opposite hand moved to cup my nape as his knees bent in a way that pushed me higher so our mouths hovered near one another. "When you go into heat in two days, I will claim you, Omega. In every way. This was just my audition."

"Audition?" I repeated.

He smiled. "Yeah. I'm courting you, remember?" The words were a breath against my lips, sending a shiver down my spine.

"I like your method of courting," I replied, my inner walls squeezing his shaft as proof. "Feel free to court me all night."

He rolled me onto my back again, one hand remaining at the nape of my neck while the other ventured up to palm my breast. "Is that an invitation to play in your nest, Daciana?"

"It's an invitation to do whatever you like," I told him, meaning it.

"That's dangerous, sweetheart. You have no idea how much I want to do to you."

Actually, I had a pretty good idea of what he desired. Which was how I knew he'd held back for our first time. "You're a worthy mate, Elias of Andorra Sector," I said, repeating my words from earlier. "I meant what I said about my estrus. I would like it to be you."

"Are you going to try to run first?" The hint of teasing in his voice told me he might enjoy that. But I knew better than to play such a dangerous game in this unknown territory.

"No," I whispered. "Because I wouldn't want to risk anyone else catching me." And someone might. Especially here, in a place where I had no known places to hide.

He grew serious, his touch lifting from my chest to my face, where his thumb drifted along my bottom lip. "No one else will touch you, Daciana. I told you—I don't share what's mine."

"I'm not yours yet," I reminded him.

Elias canted his head, a devious twinkle in his gaze. "Oh, darling, you were mine the moment I took you into my lair. Everyone knows. And in two days, I'll make it permanent." He released my face and palmed my belly. "We're going to create the future together, Omega. The first Ash and X-Clan hybrid."

"Assuming I'm compatible." Something we didn't yet know for sure. "We don't even know if you can claim me as a mate." Just the thought soured my stomach. Because if Elias couldn't mark me as his, then I'd be sent back to Shadowlands Sector.

Ice drizzled through my veins.

I didn't want to go home.

Because I didn't have one.

I wanted Elias to become mine. To stay with him. To be chosen. To mate. To create a future, just like he said.

"Shh," Elias hushed, his purr-like vibration surrounding me once more. "We'll figure this out, sweetheart. Don't give up before we've even started." His knot dislodged, causing me to feel empty inside.

He slipped out of me, our joined pleasure seeping between my legs.

No sign of life pulsated within me.

No baby in my abdomen.

Not that there should be one; I wasn't in heat yet.

But what happened if the same sensation hit me in four or five days when I surfaced from estrus? Would I find myself unclaimed? Alone all over again?

The very prospect lashed at my heart.

At some point, I'd decided on Elias becoming mine, a hazardous decision when I had no choices in this world. And this one in particular could so easily be ripped from my grasp.

Elias's reverberations heightened, his lips tracing my damp cheeks. *I'm crying*, I realized. The thought of him not being mine had reduced me to tears.

"Come now, let's head back to the dome and have some dinner. You'll feel better afterward. Then maybe you can invite me into your nest." He nuzzled my neck and brushed his lips over mine. "Okay?"

I swallowed, a lump clogging my throat. All I could do was nod.

Worrying myself accomplished nothing. I knew that. He knew that. Only time could tell us what fate had in store.

For now, I had to keep moving. Focus on my purpose. Seek the truth with my chosen Alpha. And play my part in this grand experiment.

If we found out I couldn't be his, I'd handle the truth then.

In the meantime, I'd work on hardening my heart. Just in case.

Only, as I followed him back to our clothes in wolf form, I found that task to be impossible. With every glance back to check on my pace, I caught the devotion in his gaze. As we both dressed, I scented his desire for me. And when we returned to the condo, I experienced what life in his arms would entail. He cuddled me on the couch, where we ate a decadent meal of savory flavors that stroked my soul. Then he took me to my nest and held me into the late hours of the night, his purr music to my ears.

Never had I felt more whole or cared for in my entire life.

Elias brought me to life in the best way.

He taught me in a few short days that I could love.

And that he might be the one my soul always dreamed about.

When Dušan sent me here, I expected to be torn apart in the lab and fucked to within an inch of my life. His people might have promised me courtship, but I'd known better than to believe them. Caspian's words from the plane on my way here were the ones I took as truth, the jokes he'd tossed around about how the Alphas would rip me apart with their knots.

Oh, I'd felt split in two by Elias. No question about that. Yet it'd been in the most delicious way. One I was dying to experience again.

I squeezed my thighs at the thought, my slick permeating the cocoon of my nest.

"You're a conundrum," Elias whispered, his chest to my back. "One moment, I scent fear and pain from you. The next, arousal. Your mind enthralls me, Daciana." His palm slid from my belly down to the place I desired him most. He hissed, his finger drawing through my folds and upward to circle my sensitive bundle of nerves. "You're drenched, darling."

His words made me even wetter, a small whimper leaving my mouth.

Never had it been like this.

Most males frightened me.

This one had me fighting my instincts, trying desperately to rein in my hormones and failing to stay dry.

"I know what you need," he continued, applying pressure to my nub. "Ride my hand, baby." His lips caressed my neck, his arousal growing against my ass.

We'd both entered my nest naked. I'd taken Elias's shirt without a word, adding it to my sanctuary before taking off his pants and setting them on the dresser. He hadn't made a move, allowing me to again lead, and just watched as I disrobed and slid into my safe haven. When I left enough room for him to enter, he joined me.

No words.

Just motions.

And I loved it. Loved that he understood me without me having to speak. That talent alone made him perfect for me.

I undulated my hips against his hand now, seeking the pleasure I craved. It was wanton and new. Satisfying, too. He hummed against my throat, whispered dirty words in my ear about how badly he wanted to knot me again, to take my ass, my mouth, any way he could, over and over again.

Each fantasy painted a vivid picture in my mind, drawing me closer to my goal.

I knew what he was doing—preparing me. Ensuring I understood exactly what he intended to do to me during my heat cycle. Guaranteeing my consent. And I adored him for that. He didn't want to surprise me, but he expected my submission, to allow him to do whatever he craved.

And I found I wanted everything he detailed.

Even the harsher descriptions.

When he talked about fucking me from behind while keeping my hands locked behind my back and my face buried in the pillows, I came. The image had hit me somewhere deep inside, the notion of giving up all my control to him, and trusting him to care for me during my weakest moment, causing me to come undone.

Because I realized I already trusted him.

A gift I'd never given to anyone, yet this male had earned it in record time.

And for that alone, I started to love him.

As I came down from my high, I turned in his arms and kissed him, allowing him to feel the emotions he awoke inside me. And as he slid his cock into my slick channel, I knew this time would be different. A slower mating. One meant for our bodies to better acquaint themselves.

I spread my legs, welcoming him, and moaned as he pushed me onto my back to settle on top of me.

His weight felt right.

His kiss perfect.

His hands roaming up and down my sides, brands that claimed me as his.

His shaft fit perfectly in my damp heat. My soreness from earlier was long gone, replaced with a knowledge of the pleasure to come.

He took me slowly and thoroughly, his knot inching higher and higher with each stroke.

We were lazily fucking.

Adoring each other.

Worshiping our joining.

Memorizing.

I arched into him and he slid deeper, caressing the part of me that brought tears to my eyes.

We didn't speak this time. There were no more dirty words. Just us, our nest, and the sounds of our bodies joining below. Another piece of my heart went to him in that moment, my soul melting into his.

Our groans mingled in the air as his knot found its home deep inside me, his seed filling my womb and bringing me to orgasm once more.

I smiled against his mouth, thriving in our joined rapture. It seduced me into a languid state, one that caused my eyes to droop until nothing but stars existed behind my lids.

Mmm, yes.

I wanted to stay here forever.

And so I did.

My consciousness slipped into a sleep state, even while he continued to come inside me. Maybe if I was lucky, he'd wake me in a similar manner.

CHAPTER EIGHT

ELIAS

"NO MORE TESTS," I said, setting my coffee mug on the counter with a finality that reverberated through my kitchen.

Ander stood across from me, his thick arms folded over his wide chest. "Ceres didn't realize how tight the straps were because she never mentioned it, E. You can't hold that against him. It's just impeding our mission."

"Our mission is to find out if she can procreate with an X-Clan Wolf, and I'll have that answer for you within the next week." I wasn't negotiating this. There would be no more experiments. No more poking and prodding. No more lab visits. "She's a wolf, Ander, not a test subject."

He blew out a breath. "Consider this from a different

angle. It's possible Ceres can do something to enhance her ability to conceive. But we won't know without more samples."

"How about we do this my way for the week, and if that doesn't work out, we discuss this further?" Whereby I'd still tell him to fuck off because she would be my mate by the end of her heat cycle, regardless of whether or not our souls joined.

The look in his gold eyes told me he saw right through me. It also said he knew this was a fight he wouldn't win, and Ander Cain always picked his battles intelligently. "You realize if you were anyone else, I'd demand you present her to Ceres within the hour, right?"

I smirked. "Careful, Cain, or I'll think you're displaying signs of gratitude."

He snorted. "You know I'm thankful for you, dipshit."

"You really do have a way with words," I teased him. "I do hope you're trying harder with your intended mate."

All signs of humor fled from his features, his lips flattening. "That would require my mate to speak to me, something she doesn't seem very fond of doing right now."

"I have no idea why," I drawled, feigning surprise. "It's not like you were an ass or anything." Impregnating her without mating her. Such a dick move.

His gaze narrowed. "You know why I did it."

"Yeah, I do. Does she?" I asked, arching a brow.

"That would defeat the purpose of the lesson."

"Yes, you're right. Communication is never a good idea." I couldn't hide my sarcasm. "Who would have thought it'd be me giving you relationship advice?"

Another snort from the Sector Alpha. "Everyone seems to think they can do this better than I can."

"Because apparently we can," I replied as Daciana entered the living area in nothing but my shirt. She kept her eyes on me, asking for approval without words. I lifted my arm, signaling for her to join me. Her lips curled slightly, her cheeks reddening, and she continued her movement forward.

Her head fit perfectly against my shoulder as she tucked herself against my side. I kissed the top of her head while Ander watched. "Good morning, princess," I murmured.

"Morning," she whispered.

"Are you hungry?"

She nodded. "Yes."

"Then it's a good thing I made eggs for three." Ander was planning to stay for breakfast because he wanted to talk to me about Daciana and her potential for mating. I'd addressed the experiment discussion first, ensuring he knew my stance. It wasn't up for debate. We would test the theories the old-fashioned way.

Grabbing plates from the cupboard, I divvied up the portions and slid them across the counter toward the dining area. Ander took my cue, making up the table with silverware from the drawers and moving the plates to the various settings. Then he grabbed our mugs and looked at Daciana. "Do you want any coffee?"

She shook her head. "No, thank you."

"Juice?" I pressed. "Milk? Water?"

"Do you have any tea?" She glanced at my stove with a hopeful look.

"I don't, but we can get you tea." Ander sourced a myriad of products from all over the world, thanks to our ability to trade in technology. The man truly was brilliant. "What kind do you like?"

Daciana listed a few flavors, and Ander sent off a message before I had a chance to bring up a screen. "Ten minutes," he said, sitting down and picking up his coffee mug.

"What is that?" my intended mate asked, staring at Ander's wrist. "I mean, I know it's a watch, but..." She canted her head, studying the device. "It's more than that."

"Much more," I agreed, pouring her a glass of water to hold her over until her tea arrived. "I have one, too," I said, rolling up the sleeve of my sweater. "It's essentially a computer in watch form. It even shifts with us when we become wolves."

Her lips parted. "How?"

"Technology is our primary export," Ander replied after taking a long sip of his coffee. "It's part of why Dušan is so eager to trade with us. Shadowlands Sector isn't as advanced as we are here."

"Understatement," Daciana muttered, taking the seat I'd pulled out for her.

I settled into the one beside her and draped my arm over the back of her chair, meeting Ander's gaze across from us. "You're the genius. Show her what your little gadget does."

He scoffed at that. "I didn't invent it."

"No, you just organized the team that did." I gave him a knowing look before switching focus to my Omega. "Don't let him fool you. He's not nearly as humble as he appears."

"Asshole," Ander muttered.

"Right back at you, dick," I returned, picking up my fork. "Now eat the food I made for you."

My oldest friend narrowed his gaze. "Don't make me remind you of your place in front of your intended. It won't be pretty."

Now it was my turn to scoff. "As if you could."

Daciana shivered beneath my arm, her gaze darting

between us with rising concern. She clearly didn't follow our sarcasm.

"He's my best friend," I informed her softly. "We frequently bicker."

"Because your intended is an ass," Ander added before shoveling a bite of eggs into his mouth. "But at least he can cook."

"Yes. It's my one redeeming quality." I toasted him with my coffee and took a sip while Daciana relaxed beside me.

"You have several redeeming qualities," she murmured. "And I don't think you're an ass at all."

My lips curled, her words warming my heart. "Thank you."

She returned my grin with a small one of her own, then began to eat.

Ander watched us in that keen way of his, a hint of agitation lining his shoulders. Not because he disapproved. No, I sensed it had something to do with the troubles between him and his intended.

Their situation was entirely different, what with the female having grown up with humans. Daciana at least understood our world and her place within it. Katriana—Ander's chosen mate—did not. And she'd proven it by trying to run several weeks ago. Hence his resulting punishment. She'd not only put his reputation on the line but also risked her own life in the process.

Foolish girl.

Stubborn, too.

He certainly had his hands full sorting that mess out.

Daciana's tea arrived from one of the Betas working in the building today. The smaller female appeared without a word, delivering a fresh cup and also stocking my cupboards with supplies for more. Ander and I thanked her with a nod while Daciana observed.

"Is she one of your lovers?" my intended asked, causing me to choke on my eggs.

"*What?*"

She nodded after the female, who had already left my condo. "The Beta. Is she one of your lovers?"

"No." I picked up my coffee to take a long sip before asking, "Why would you think that?"

"You said I met a few yesterday. I wondered if she was one, too."

Ander arched a brow at me. "Who did she meet?"

"Sly and Candice while I gave her a tour of the town," I replied. Neither one of them was women we'd ever shared, which I suspected was why he asked. "I explained to Daciana that our Beta females voluntarily service Alphas in this sector."

"I would go as far as to say they enjoy it," he replied, shrugging a shoulder. "They're paid well, kept in beautiful homes, and they dictate their limits. Morgana, who just delivered your tea, is a member of the building's staff. She's happily married to a Beta male who works in one of the technical labs. Everyone in Andorra has a job, including our Omegas, but it's of their choosing. Never by force."

"So your Beta females enjoy being used sexually by your Alphas?" she countered, a hint of derision underlining her tone.

"Daciana," I warned. She couldn't speak to the Sector Alpha in that manner, not without provoking retaliation.

"It's just, in my experience, females are often forced into that profession for lack of other opportunities." She dared to meet Ander's gaze while she spoke, her defiance outlined in the tensing of her jaw.

He stared her down, unflinching. "Your experience is limited," he replied.

"I grew up in a whore's house," she countered.

Ander growled, both in response to her continued disobedience and the term she'd chosen. I tightened my hold around her. "Careful, Daciana. He might be my best friend, but he's also the Sector Alpha."

"I'm aware of your history, Daciana, which is why I'm going to let the accusation in your tone slide. But you should be mindful of the fact that I'm your Sector Alpha now, not Dušan. You should show me the same respect you would show him."

"I never met Dušan," she replied.

"And yet, I imagine that if you did, you would never have spoken to him the way you are to me right now," he retorted, a note of reprimand underlining his words.

She swallowed, her gaze finally dropping as she chewed the inside of her cheek. "No. No, I wouldn't."

"Then I should be no different," Ander pressed, driving his point home.

Her blonde head bobbed as an apology fell from her lips, one that hurt my heart. Was she out of line? Yes. But I also understood why.

"Sly, who you met yesterday, is a lab technician," I explained softly. "She chooses to play with Alphas on the weekend because she likes pleasure."

"And Candice often helps Riley with organizing the pharmaceutical supplies because she was a pharmacist before the world collapsed into chaos," Ander added. "She, too, only indulges on the weekends, because she hasn't found a Beta who suits her preferences."

Daciana blinked. "So they have choices."

"Yes," Ander confirmed. "Everyone in my sector has the opportunity to pick their professional path. I just ask that they give back to our society in some way."

"And your Omegas?" she asked, lifting her gaze again, this time in a less bold manner. "What do they do?"

"Riley is a physician, which you know. Many of the others prefer to raise children as their primary responsibility, but some maintain positions. Alyona, for example, is a teacher." He studied her. "Is there something you would enjoy doing in Andorra, Daciana? A trade you bring with you that may be useful or enjoyable for you to pursue?"

"Other than mating?" she asked.

Ander nodded. "Yes."

"Isn't it a moot point? If I'm not a viable candidate for procreation, you'll just send me back. Why bother discussing what I could offer beyond that?" I could tell by her tone that she hadn't meant that to come off as hostile as it sounded, more so curious.

"Humor me," Ander replied. "Let's assume your mating with Elias goes as hoped. What then would you like to do here?"

She glanced at me, then back at the Sector Alpha, and then back at me again. "I…" She licked her lips, twisting them slightly to the side. "Well, I'm quite skilled with a bow. I could hunt."

My eyebrows shot up.

I never would have anticipated *that* as her reply.

Not because I doubted her or thought it a humorous answer.

Quite the opposite, actually.

"Huh," Ander said, picking up his coffee, amusement in his gaze. "Perhaps she is your soul mate after all."

"No 'perhaps' about it," I countered, staring at her in awe. "I'm the Andorra Commander because of my skill with never missing a target." I mostly used guns now, the technology far more advanced and faster on the trigger, but I used to be quite handy with a bow back in the day.

"You should take her to the range. See how she does," Ander suggested.

I smiled. "Yeah. I think we'll do exactly that."

"Range?" she repeated, glancing between us once more.

"A place to practice shooting." I nodded at her plate. "Finish your eggs and we'll go." We still had a few days before the full moon. Might as well continue her introduction to our world here in the interim.

Ander gave a subtle nod in approval.

Not surprising since he'd been the one to accept the courting clause in Dušan's agreement.

I'd report back to him later with anything of value, including an evaluation of her skill with a bow. We didn't need a hunter—we sourced most of our food from other sectors—but I could always use a skilled sharpshooter. Whether it be to help protect our home or to teach others, maybe even our youth, remained to be seen. There was no way I would send her on a mission with my men. However, there were other ways she could be useful to my unit.

I smiled. "You continue to surprise me, Daciana of Shadowlands Sector."

She looked at me, her blue eyes sparkling with a hint of happiness. "You continue to surprise me, too, Elias of Andorra Sector."

CHAPTER NINE

ELIAS

ANOTHER BULL'S-EYE.

I blew out a breath and shook my head. "You weren't kidding about being good with a bow." Even with the high-tech one I'd fitted for her, she nailed every target.

"These are so much better than the ones I used to make back home," she said, stroking the metal tips of the traceability arrows I favored. Striking a target with one of these allowed us to track them across the globe, assuming the victim survived. The heads used nanotechnology to infiltrate the blood of the victim.

Absolutely brilliant, but not necessarily useful in our new era. At least not in Andorra.

I handed her a pistol next, curious to see how her skill translated to firearms.

It took a bit to explain how to operate the machinery, then I fitted her with protective headgear and watched as she familiarized herself with the weapon. She didn't catch on immediately, but after two hours of experimenting, she fell into a rhythm and started hitting her targets with unerring accuracy.

A natural.

Her smile was brilliant when she finished, her blue eyes glowing. "This would be far more useful in the wild."

"Hmm, yet nothing beats the excitement of a bow," I mused.

She agreed, handing me the weapon. "Efficiency trumps excitement in most situations."

"True." I showed her how to take apart the gun next before introducing her to other higher-tech items. Daciana observed with an eagerness that thrilled me. Most females chose not to play in the weapons range. Meanwhile, it seemed my intended was born for it.

We'd definitely have to find her an appropriate role, one that kept her out of harm's way while allowing her to flourish.

Being an Omega marked her as naturally weaker, something no amount of weapons could change. Putting her in the field was never going to happen. Not to mention my instinct to protect her would make enjoyment for either of us impossible in that realm. So we'd determine another way for her to be involved.

"You're in charge of all this?" she asked as I stowed the weapons we'd used today.

"Yes. As Ander's Second, I am in charge of defense and security for the sector." It also suited my enforcer background and general affinity for military intelligence and strategy.

"Which is why everyone calls you Commander," she

said, glancing around the range and noting all the males at attention nearby. They would remain that way until I left, their obedience resolute regardless of whether or not I told them to stand down. In the comfort of a bar or a less professional arena, they would relax. But not on these grounds, where I functioned as their Alpha and lead lieutenant.

Ander often joked that they would probably take my word as law over his.

He wasn't wrong.

I slipped my hand into hers, tugging her away from the range and toward my office at the edge of the base. While here, I might as well check in to make sure everything was running as expected. We rarely had issues, just the occasional hiccups—like humans trying to attack our food shipments.

Idiots.

Daciana kept her gaze averted while we walked, her submissive Omega qualities on full display. Most of the men around the base were Alphas, their interest in her implied through their scent. However, they knew better than to try to talk to her or touch her. I might not have marked her or claimed her yet, but my intent was clear in the way I held her close. She was also wearing one of my shirts with the jeans she'd borrowed from Riley.

Her lack of availability was starkly evident.

And anyone who thought to question it could answer directly to me.

I led her to a sofa inside my office, then went to my desk to review the notes Jaxon had left for me. Nothing pertinent, which didn't surprise me. He would have called if he needed me to handle anything.

"Do your weapons work on the Infected?" Daciana asked after several minutes of silence.

"They do."

She nodded. "But you need to be in human form to use them. So if they come across you as wolves, they can still bite."

"They could, yeah. Except we run a lot faster than they do."

"Yes," she agreed, seeming to relax. "Yes, we do."

"There are weapons stashed all over Andorra," I told her after a beat, realizing her fear. "I'll show you where some of them are on our next run so if an Infected is ever on your tail, you'll know where to go." Not that she'd ever be running without me by her side. Well, not anytime soon, anyway. I didn't trust the other wolves to leave her alone without me nearby.

Case in point, the approaching scent of a male I knew wouldn't leave her alone regardless of whether I stood in the same room or not.

"Ah, I thought I smelled something that didn't belong," Artur murmured, entering without knocking.

Daciana stiffened on the couch while I openly ignored him.

"Shouldn't the lab rat be with Ceres?" Artur continued, his tone underlined in disdain. "Or have you brought her here for us to sample the wares?"

My jaw tightened at the very prospect of that happening. "She's mine."

"Yours?" Artur started toward her. "Odd. I don't smell a claiming bond."

I pushed away from my desk and stepped in front of him, blocking his view of Daciana. "What do you want, Artur?"

"To see what all the fuss is about, of course. If Ander expects us to start fucking Ash Wolves, I'd like to taste the sample we were offered. As you've already done the same, I'm sure you understand."

"She's not available," I said without inflection. "So

kindly fuck off."

He narrowed his gaze. "Not available because Ander gave you first dibs."

I didn't dignify that with a reply.

It had nothing to do with Ander or his loyalty to me and everything to do with my position in the sector. I *earned* first dibs by being stronger and faster than all the other Alphas in this territory. If he wanted to challenge that, he was more than welcome to try.

"The least you could do is share," Artur murmured, cocking his head to the side. "Think of it as a way to prove to us all that Ash Wolf pussy is worth the trouble."

I folded my arms. "Even if I was going to share her— which I'm not—it would never be with you."

He growled low in his throat, the insult cutting through his elegant exterior. "Careful, Elias, or I'll begin to take this conversation personally."

"It was personal the moment you walked into my office without so much as a knock," I countered.

"As I said, I was following the scent of something *wrong*."

"Leave, Artur."

Daciana whimpered behind me, her body reacting to the heat of two angry Alphas. Artur's nostrils flared, intrigue darkening his gaze. He growled again, this time at a lower level, invoking his mating call.

My intended's hard limit.

I slammed my fist into his face and backed him out of my office before shoving him into the wall. "She isn't yours."

"She isn't yours either," he snarled, grabbing me by the collar of my shirt. "I'm not going to fight with you over some trailer trash from Romania."

"Then I suggest you unhand me and walk away because I *will* kick your ass if you say one more negative word about my intended mate." I shoved him away from me with enough force to make him stumble. "You don't stand a chance here, old man. Walk away while you can." Because I would destroy him if he so much as grumbled again.

He spit out a mouthful of blood, my punch having done more damage than I thought.

I wasn't sorry.

"You and Ander are making a mistake by trying to force these Ash Wolves down our throats," he snapped. "They're inferior to our bloodlines and unworthy of our seed."

"Yet you wanted to sample my intended just moments ago," I drawled. "Make up your fucking mind and get out of my face."

"I didn't say their pussies were completely useless. They can still accept the knot. But I'll die before I mate one."

"I'll happily ensure that happens for you sooner rather than later," I offered conversationally. "Just give me a date, Artur. I'll have your grave ready."

Aggression poured off him.

I readied my stance, just in case he decided to do something reckless like charge me.

"When she proves useless and incompatible, send her my way," he finally said, choosing to save face through unveiled insults. "I could use a good Omega fuck."

I snorted. "Yeah. Sure." That would never happen. Even if Daciana proved incompatible, he'd be the last one I'd ever give her to. His lack of respect for females in this sector was well known, hence him actually believing I might give him my Omega after I finished.

Fucking prick.

"Anything else?" I asked, arching a brow.

He shook his head. "It won't work."

"We'll see," I replied.

"Yes. We will," he agreed, a knowing gleam in his gaze.

I left him in the hall, shutting my office door to make a point that I was done with our conversation. If he chose to reenter, I'd drive that point home in a very different manner.

Clicking a button on my watch, I pulled up a screen and sent a quick note to Ander about Artur's behavior. It wouldn't shock him, but the incident needed to be documented. The much older shifter was growing ballsier by the day. I wouldn't be surprised if he or his buddy Enzo challenged Ander for leadership again soon.

It was usually the latter—Enzo, the stronger Alpha of the two.

But something about Artur's behavior lately suggested he might be the one to take a shot at it next.

Regardless, the two assholes would fail. The only one in this sector who might win a challenge against Ander was me, and that would never happen. I had no desire to lead and we both knew it.

Running my fingers through my hair, I took in Daciana's frozen form on the sofa. She was practically vibrating with fear.

Artur's growl, I realized, sighing.

Crouching down before her, I tried to meet her gaze, but she refused to look at me. "Hey," I said softly. "He's gone. It's okay." I reached out to run my knuckles along her cheek, and she flinched away from me, her blue irises flashing up to mine.

"You lied to me."

I frowned. "No, I didn't."

"You said you wouldn't share me."

"And I won't."

She pointed at the door, her ire fanning her features

in a deep red. "You just told that male he could have me when you were done."

"No, I…" I trailed off, considering what she'd heard.

She chose that moment to jump off the couch and round on me. "You're just like the Alphas back home! Using females for pleasure because they're unable or unworthy of giving you more!" Her palm slapped against my chest, her fury coating the air. "Ash Wolves might be built differently, but we're not beneath you. We're… we're… we're special in our own way. And maybe I don't want to be compatible with your X-Clan seed. Maybe I don't even want to be here!"

I let her rant.

Accepted the hits to my chest.

As she continued to scream about the differences between us and how they were irrelevant. How wolves were wolves. How maybe the Infected could turn her, but that didn't make her inferior. How she didn't smell wrong. How she was worth more than her ability to procreate. How she didn't need a mate. How she never asked for any of this. How terrified she was that I might not be able to claim her.

And inevitably, how she didn't mean any of it at all, that the idea of not being able to give me a child made her feel inferior and weak.

Her anger melted into a sob, and I caught her as her knees gave out beneath her.

I pulled her into my arms to kiss away her tears.

My strong Omega was afraid.

She'd hidden it well, but I sensed it beneath the surface, and now she let me see it all. Her intrinsic fear that I'd send her back, or worse, give her to a male like Artur. That her entire existence was designed for failure. How she didn't like feeling so dependent on our mating but didn't know how else to feel.

How she worried I would discard her for another, more worthy Omega later in life.

An X-Clan Omega who had the right genetics to provide what I truly craved.

I lifted her into my arms and sat with her on the sofa, holding her tightly as I unleashed a rumble from my chest that I knew would calm her.

She squirmed and I held her tighter.

She cried and I kissed away her tears.

All the while, I purred, soothing her.

Until, eventually, she began to still.

"Daciana," I whispered, my lips near her ear. "We don't know yet what the future holds. But I promise you, I will never allow a male like Artur to touch you. Ever."

She shook her head sadly. "I heard what you said."

"It was sarcasm, sweetheart." I combed my fingers through her hair, revealing her sweet face and guiding her watery eyes to mine. "It was meant to be a derogatory reply, not to you but to him." I pinched her chin, needing her to hear my next words. "Just the notion of sharing you infuriates me, Daciana. I will murder anyone who touches you. Do you understand?"

I allowed her to see the truth in my gaze, aware that my wolf stared down at her now. *He* would rip the offender to shreds.

"You're mine," I added, unable to help the growl in my tone. "*Mine*, Daciana."

CHAPTER TEN

DACIANA

ELIAS'S PROCLAMATION SHIVERED OVER ME, his words singeing my very spirit.

Despite the words I'd overheard from the hallway, I believed him. Fury pulsed through him, the very idea that someone else might take me causing him to tighten his grip to a near-painful level.

Because he didn't want to share me.

And that male—*Artur*—had spoken out of line.

"Yeah. Sure." Elias's words played over and over through my head, the inflection behind them, the scent of irritation surrounding him.

Sarcasm.

I understood the concept but rarely experienced it.

He'd meant it to be rude, to rival the ill-mannered behavior of the other Alpha.

"Yours," I agreed slowly, staring deeply into his eyes that had gone wolfish on me. While the male held me, it was his wolf talking to me now. He'd even growled. And oddly, I hadn't minded.

I captured his mouth with my own, kissing him.

He granted me the first touch of our tongues, then took over on a groan I felt between my legs. His hands fell to my hips as I straddled him, my arms wrapping around his neck.

My heat cycle wouldn't begin for another day or two, yet my core dampened in preparation, reminding me of my estrus.

No other male had ever provoked this response in me.

Until Elias.

He pulled my shirt over my head, exposing my breasts. His mouth sealed around one nipple, then the other, his teeth grazing my sensitive skin and shrouding my body in anticipatory goose bumps.

I tugged at his hair.

Growled for more.

Craving his bite.

Oh, I was so gone to this man.

My Alpha.

My Elias.

He rotated until my back hit the cushion of the couch, his much larger form looming over me. "I'm going to fuck you, Daciana," he said. "And you're going to scream so loud that everyone in this fucking quadrant is going to hear you."

He flicked open my jeans.

Drew down the zipper.

And inhaled deeply.

"They'll all know it's me inside your sweet cunt, darling. Owning you. Possessing you. *Claiming* you."

"Yes," I hissed, lifting my hips to help him remove my jeans.

"They'll know by the end how worthy you are," he continued, his nose skimming from my knees up to my inner thigh. "How Ash Wolf Omegas are just as beautiful and amazing as X-Clan Omegas. And they'll envy me for taking you, baby." He spoke the final words directly above my heated flesh, his breath taunting my sensitive bundle of nerves.

"Elias," I breathed, threading my fingers through his hair.

"You're mine," he said, his lips vibrating my wet folds. His tongue dipped inside, licking me deep and forcing me to bow off the cushions in wanton need.

More slick spilled from me, directly into his mouth as he devoured me in a manner I'd only ever dreamed about.

Heaven, I thought. *This is heaven.*

His mouth.

His tongue.

His *teeth*.

Oh, dear God, I couldn't breathe. Tears of a very different nature fell from my eyes. This male was wicked. Talented. Perfect. Destroying me for anyone else. And I couldn't complain. Because he'd finally introduced me to pleasure. *Real* pleasure. The kind that female wolves wished for but rarely experienced. At least in my life.

I fell in love with him a little more, my soul weaving with his in a matrimony soon to come.

All concerns of our differences fled.

Our fates intertwined.

He would claim me. I felt it all the way to my bones. Just as I knew I'd bear him a child. One with dark hair like his own and blue eyes like mine.

I smiled, arching into him once more, my lower belly clenching almost painfully. "Close," I managed to say on an exhale, my pulse racing in my ears.

"Mmm, I know," he murmured, his eyes lifting to mine. "Scream for me, princess. Scream my name."

He sealed his mouth around my clit, sucking hard and demanding I orgasm in response.

So I did.

I gave him everything.

My heart.

My breath.

My very soul.

His name left my mouth on a chant, my limbs shaking, my vision blurring, my entire body *singing* for his.

And then he was there, sliding into me, his jeans unfastened but still encasing his legs. The abrasion irritated my upper thighs, but I welcomed the distraction, allowing it to pull me back to reality just enough to feel every inch of his entry.

"This is going to hurt," he warned me.

I welcomed him with a sigh, my nails biting into the back of his neck as his mouth aggressively took mine.

My arousal coated his tongue, elevating me to new heights as he fucked me *hard*.

So much harder than before.

Fast.

Violent.

As if he were channeling all of his residual frustration from the confrontation into each thrust of his hips against mine.

I took it.

Accepted it.

Reveled in it.

Because through the pain, a maelstrom of sensation began to build, all culminating in the sensitive space between my thighs.

Each drive forward stoked my inner flame.

Every drag of his teeth along my lip and tongue intensified our joining.

And the delicious feel of his pants abrading my sensitive flesh had me crying out for more.

His hands gripped my hips, angling me to receive him deeper. He would leave bruises. I'd wear them with pride.

We were positively savage in our need, my walls clamping down around him, demanding he take me harder. His mouth claiming mine with a brutality that nearly drew blood. And our lower bodies slamming together in a frantic pace that left me unable to breathe.

Not that it mattered.

I was too busy screaming anyway.

My voice had gone hoarse, my fingers aching from how hard I clutched him. Until I couldn't take it anymore and tumbled into rapture ahead of him, my inner channel squeezing him and demanding he follow.

Elias groaned my name, low and deep, then roared as he claimed me from the inside, his seed spilling heavily into me with the release of his knot.

It invoked a whole new wave of pleasure inside me, sending me spiraling for a third time as moisture poured from my eyes.

I panted, my chest burning with the need for oxygen, my heart beating at an unhealthy rhythm.

The scent of iron told me one or both of us was bleeding.

I licked my bottom lip, tasting it.

Swallowing.

I shook beneath him, feeling amazingly used and absolutely full of *him*. My mate. My Elias. He still hadn't bitten me. Not the way he needed to. But I felt his intention in the way he held me, the look in his eyes, and the throb of his cock between my legs.

He already considered me his.

And in a few days' time, he'd finalize it for us both.

Just as soon as I went into heat.

I didn't ask why he hadn't tried today or last night. Although, I probably should have. But a part of me didn't want to ask because I already knew.

He wouldn't claim a female he couldn't impregnate.

No Alpha would.

My heart sank with the knowledge, but I swallowed back the emotion, understanding the practicality of our situation.

He deserved a mate who could bear him a child.

I just needed to ensure I could be that mate.

I will be, I thought. *I have to be.*

Because just like Elias, I had no intention of ever sharing him with another. Except he already had others. Betas.

I frowned.

How could a male be mine when he played with others?

"That is not the look of a satisfied female," Elias whispered, his eyes on me, like they always were. So in tune with my every emotion and thought. "Tell me what gave you that expression and don't lie."

"It's nothing," I said, my voice scratchy from screaming so intently.

"Lie," he accused, rotating us to our sides with his rear facing the room and my back pressed up against the couch, effectively caging me. "Answer me, Daciana." He pulled my leg over his thigh, keeping us locked together intimately while he continued to spill inside me. "Now."

I bristled beneath his command. Not only did he have me in an inferior position, but he was also using his dominance against me in voice. "You have other lovers," I stated flatly. "The thought of them made me frown. Just as I'm sure you would frown if *I* had other lovers, but I'll never have them, will I?"

He reared back as if I'd slapped him. "Do you want other lovers?"

"No," I snapped. "It'd just be... I don't..." I growled, irritated. "You ruined a perfectly nice moment, and I can't even leave because, well." I rotated my hips, then groaned at how that felt.

Damn Alpha knot!

His expression morphed into one of amusement as a chuckle tickled his chest. "You're adorable when flustered, Daciana."

"And you're irritating when... when... well, right now," I replied, my fight deflating at how ridiculous I sounded. "Never mind." I buried my face against his shirt—or tried to, anyway. His palm caught my nape and dragged me back, forcing me to look at him and his damn infuriating smile.

"You're jealous."

I rolled my eyes and didn't dignify that statement with a response. He'd be jealous, too, if the roles were reversed.

No, actually, he'd go on a murderous rampage.

Unless he really did want to share me.

I shook my head, refuting that thought. *No.* I felt how much he did not want to share me. The soreness between my thighs proved it.

"They're my *former* lovers, Daciana," Elias said, tightening his grip. "As in, my past. *You* are my future."

"Unless I can't bear you an heir," I reminded him.

He growled in reply, then immediately stopped and cursed. "I'm sorry." He pressed his forehead to mine. "I'm sorry, Daciana."

It took me a moment to understand why he was apologizing. Then my eyes widened. *He takes me seriously.* I already knew that, of course. But to feel his contriteness over *growling* had me gazing at him in a whole new light.

What was more, his growl hadn't bothered me.

If anything, I'd *liked* it because it vibrated the place we were joined.

"Do it again," I whispered, losing focus on our conversation and staring deep into his dark eyes. "Growl again."

"What?"

"Please. I want... I need to see something." I swallowed. "Do a mating growl. Just a soft one."

"Daciana..."

"Just one," I implored him.

He studied me for a long moment, then conceded with a subtle, soft growl that went straight to my clit. I jolted against him, my body shaking as a fresh surge of wetness coated the cock lodged deep inside me. "*Ohhh,*" I whispered, shuddering. "*Oh,* I liked that."

Another growl followed, this one stronger, the vibration rocking me from head to toe.

I grabbed his shoulders, holding on tight as another of those amazing trembles overtook me.

"Again," I breathed, my thigh over his legs squeezing in an attempt to drive him into me.

"I can't," he whispered. "Not until my knot is ready again."

A growl of my own vibrated us both, earning me a chuckle from the Alpha.

"Fuck, you're perfect," he marveled, his thumb brushing the column of my neck as he angled my head upward to meet his kiss.

Soft, plump lips captured mine, his tongue slowly entering my mouth to lay claim all over again. I groaned, losing myself to him completely.

Whatever he said, it didn't matter.

Whatever our future held, I didn't care.

This moment, being with him, provided me with more happiness than my entire lifetime. For that, I would forever be grateful to him.

We kissed for minutes, maybe even hours, allowing our bodies to do the talking for us. And when it was finally time for him to take me again, he growled. Not harshly. Not demandingly. Just a subtle, warm noise that sealed my fate.

I belonged to him.

Heart, body, and soul.

His.

And the way he took me told me he knew it, too.

CHAPTER ELEVEN

ELIAS

"SHE'S FERTILE," Ceres reported at the head of the council table, his voice devoid of emotion. "But we won't know if she's a hospitable host until after her estrus is complete."

Which should begin tomorrow or the following day at the latest since her heat cycle was based on the full moon.

"How convenient," Enzo drawled.

Artur snorted beside him. "We should do this like the old times—put her in a room, let the Alphas have her. The strongest of us will plant a seed."

"More likely she won't conceive at all," Enzo argued. "In which case we could at least say we all tried rather than leaving it in the hands of Elias. We don't even know if he's capable of impregnating an Omega."

My eyebrows shot up.

But it was Ander who replied, "Actually, we do. Ceres tested him, and he's a viable candidate for this job."

Having my sperm discussed so openly caused my molars to grind together in annoyance. Of course, having my intended mate's internal organs displayed across every screen in the room was far worse. They'd taken away any and every ounce of privacy she could ever think to possess and had given all the Alphas in this room her test results. Photos, too.

It made my stomach churn.

At least she wasn't here. I could only imagine her reaction—she'd shut down. Remain silent as ever. Observing without a sound. Analyzing. Listening. All the while contemplating her worth as a group of males discussed her viability for mating.

A week ago, I understood this mission.

Today, I loathed it.

"He hasn't claimed her," Artur added. "I see no reason why we can't all be provided with a chance to see if she'll accept our seed during her estrus. If she's anything like the Omegas in Andorra, she won't mind."

A handful of growls met that remark—all of them belonged to the mated Alphas in the room.

Artur merely smirked in reply. "You think we don't hear your mates in the throes of passion? That we don't smell them?"

"Are you trying to get yourself killed?" I wondered out loud. "Because I'm rather certain provoking a mated Alpha is the equivalent to begging for a death sentence."

He smiled. "You wouldn't know, now would you?"

"Yes, why haven't you tried to mate the girl?" Enzo pressed. "Too concerned that she might not provide you with an heir? Don't want to waste your bite on someone so unworthy?"

"Enough," Ander cut in, his growl resolute.

But on this, I wanted to speak. "No, I need to answer that."

His golden irises flared as he met my gaze and held it. I didn't back down.

The council needed my reason, or they'd believe Enzo's idiotic explanation. And Daciana deserved better than that. It had nothing to do with what she could provide for me and everything to do with what I could give her.

Ander gave a subtle nod.

He already knew this part, having asked me a similar question shortly after retrieving me from my den this morning. Jonas had been with him, the Alpha male agreeing to stand outside my door to guard my intended.

Of course, the only males I feared harming her were in this very room. However, given their proclivity for recruiting minions to do their dirty work, I had to be certain Daciana was safe.

"Well?" Enzo prompted. "Did you have something to say to that, *Commander*?" His derisive tone did not go unnoticed, but I chose not to rise to the bait. It was what he wanted, and we had more important items to discuss.

"The reason I haven't tried to claim her yet is that I don't wish to tie her to me if I can't provide her with a child. We all know how important procreation is to an Omega. To take away her ability to become a mother would be a cruel, unnecessary fate. And as much as I want to claim her as mine, as much as I feel she already *is* mine, I won't do that to her."

Artur huffed a laugh. "See, even Elias doesn't think she's a viable candidate."

"I didn't say that."

"Your words implied it," he countered.

"No. My words imply I'm a man of honor who doesn't wish to treat an Omega as a fucking science experiment. She's a beautiful female who deserves a future, even if I'm not the one who can give her that." The words hurt to say, my attachment to her already ingrained inside my soul. But I couldn't be a male who tied a female to him out of pure selfish need. It wouldn't be fair to her.

Ander didn't agree with my choice, and his expression said as much now.

But this wasn't his life or his decision. It was mine.

"Well, I hold no such issue with tying an Omega to me for the pure use of fucking," Enzo chimed in. "Let me have her and see what happens when I bite her."

I growled low, my warning vibrating the entire room. "You don't even want an Ash Wolf. Said they're too impure for your tastes."

"I don't know. The scent she gave off from your office yesterday certainly seemed enticing enough," Artur inserted. "Wouldn't mind a taste of that sweet Omega pussy myself."

I stood, my chair flying into the wall.

Ander was there a second later, his palm on my chest, holding me at bay.

"Stand down," he ordered, the words harsh and causing my teeth to grind together once more.

He was right.

I knew he was right.

But fuck if I wanted to *stand down*. I wanted to beat the shit out of Enzo, whip that fucking smirk off his fucking face and kick his fucking ass.

It was exactly what he wanted.

If we got into a brawl now, I'd likely be out of commission for a day or two and lose my chance with Daciana.

Then Artur would likely step into my place as the third-highest-ranking official in the dome.

No fucking way could I allow that to happen.

"Is there anything else of importance to discuss, Ceres?" Ander asked, still standing with his palm against my chest. The two of us were essentially lording over the table as a result, with the physician as the only other one on his feet in the room.

"Her genetic panels are almost identical to ours, with the exception of two genes. I suspect one of those is tied to the Ash Wolf weakness against the Infected."

That gave me pause and piqued my interest. "Can you isolate it and potentially make her immune?"

Ceres's bright green eyes locked on mine. "Yes. With more tests." It was precisely worded, but I didn't miss the jab in that phrase.

"It's something we can discuss after her estrus," Ander wisely stated.

Because he knew if everything went according to plan, she'd be my mate by the end, thus affording her higher status. It would be my decision at that point if anyone was allowed to touch my mate. And I'd be asking Daciana for her input on that choice.

"If one is tied to the Infected, what is the other mutation?" Samuel asked. The wolf notoriously sided with Enzo and Artur, but he seemed genuinely curious. As a researcher himself, I supposed he would be.

"I'm unsure because my samples are incomplete." Another jab from Ceres.

"Considering you took several pints of blood and an ungodly amount of other fluids, I would think you'd have more than enough to work with, *Doctor*," I put in.

His lip curled into a snarl.

I returned the gesture, not at all intimidated by the damn Beta.

"Right. Well, as I said, we can table this discussion for after her estrus," Ander reiterated, his hand radiating caution against my chest. "As per the agreement with the Shadowlands Sector Alpha, Elias has courted the Omega and won her favor. She asked him to see her through her cycle personally, and so he shall. There will be no old methods applied to this situation." That last part was aimed at Enzo and Artur.

They both scoffed, shaking their heads.

"And here I thought you favored diplomacy, Cain," Enzo said snidely.

"I do." Ander smiled. "We already voted on the agreement, it passed, and part of the requirements included the courting. Which is being done. End of discussion."

Artur merely stared at him, defiance written into his features.

I added weapons to my preparation list for tomorrow, as it seemed I was going to need them.

Ander dismissed the council shortly after, stating we would regroup in a week with my findings. The whole thing made my stomach hurt.

"She's more than an experiment," I told him as he followed me back up to my suite.

"I know."

"Do you?" I countered. "I get how important this deal is, I do, but she's just as precious as your Omega. And you would never allow them to talk about Katriana in this manner."

"Yet they do anyway," he replied, glancing at me. "It's the nature of the game, Elias. You know that. Enzo and Artur have been after my seat for decades. They always lose, but it doesn't stop them from being assholes."

"They don't even want Daciana," I muttered, running my fingers through my hair as the elevator doors opened.

Jonas stood against the wall, hands in his pockets, his expression bored as ever. His ice-blue eyes trailed over us, his lips twisting. "Well. Seems I didn't miss anything interesting."

"Were you expecting blood?" I wondered out loud, grinning at my favorite soldier. He used to serve for the Iceland Crisis Response Unit when the country still existed. *Badass* didn't even begin to cover it.

"Given the way Enzo and Artur have been acting since Katriana arrived, yeah, I sort of did." He pushed off the wall. "I believe your intended mate is trying to make breakfast. You may want to stop her while you still can."

My lips curled. "That bad, huh?"

"I don't think she's used to our technical advances" was all he said before stepping into the elevator we'd just vacated. "Let me know if you need me to play guard this week."

The doors closed, leaving me alone with Ander once more.

"Do you think Enzo or Artur will try anything?" I asked him.

"They'd be suicidal to attempt interfering. That said, they seem to be pushing all the boundaries lately."

"They're up to something," I agreed, my nose twitching at the scent of something burning. "Hmm." I fished my keys out of my pocket and opened the door to my condo as a curse dropped in the kitchen.

Ander followed me with an amused look.

And we paused on the threshold to see my future mate waving her hand around and a piece of black toast on the ground. "Your toaster is trying to kill me!" she accused, blowing on her fingers—fingers that were bright red with a recent burn.

I turned on the water, ensuring it was lukewarm, and

grabbed her wrist to guide her offended digits beneath the calming flow.

She hissed at first, then sighed, melting into me.

All she wore was another of my shirts, the fabric hitting her at her knees.

I'd ordered clothes for her, but they hadn't arrived yet. With my luck, they'd appear tomorrow—when we no longer needed them.

"How about you keep your hand here, and I make breakfast?" I offered, kissing her temple.

"That's my cue to stay," Ander said, popping his hip against the counter.

I flashed him a look. "Or an invitation to leave," I retorted.

"Nope. Pretty sure you want me to stay." He picked up a mug and twirled it in his hand. "I'll make coffee."

"Don't you have an intended mate to go piss off?"

"Thoroughly accomplished, my friend," he replied, bending to pick up the burnt toast and toss it into the trash can.

"You're avoiding her," I realized.

"Not exactly." He started my coffee maker, effectively ending the conversation.

Fine. If he didn't want to talk about his issues with Kat, then I'd leave him to it.

"Breakfast, but then you're going back to your kitten," I told him.

He snorted. "Well, she certainly has claws."

"I bet she does." I kissed Daciana's cheek before checking her hand and finding her skin already healing. Being a shifter certainly had perks. "Do you want some tea?"

She shook her head. "I already made some." She pointed at the pot on the table. "I was just trying to make some toast to go with it when your toaster attacked me."

I smiled. "Yeah, it does a lot more than brown bread." I'd have to show her how to use it later. "Let's try waffles instead."

"Waffles?" She scrunched her nose. "I've never had one."

"Then you're in for a treat because my *toaster* makes excellent waffles." I waggled my brows, causing her lips to twitch upward. "Go have a seat. I'll whip some up for all three of us, since Ander's invited himself to stay."

"Consider it research," he said, pouring two cups of coffee and handing one to me. "Relationship research."

"Uh-huh." More like relationship avoidance. Whatever he had going on with Kat, it was wreaking havoc on him and he craved the distraction. As he clearly didn't want to talk about it, I allowed him his diversion and busied myself with making breakfast.

He'd figure out his shit eventually.

Just as I'd figure out mine.

Daciana smiled from the table, her small hands clasped around her mug.

I returned the gesture, feeling more at home than I ever had.

The idea of her not being a compatible match had my heart stalling inside my chest, the notion of having to let her go stealing my breath. It was the right thing to do, but watching her now, I wondered if I'd actually be able to follow through. Because the very idea of another male touching her—Ash Wolf or otherwise—had me wanting to commit murder.

I gripped the counter, my back thankfully to Daciana and Ander.

Pull yourself together, I thought, closing my eyes and inhaling deeply. *You don't know the future. Take it one day at a time.*

With that mantra repeating in my head, I finished

assembling the plates, grabbed the syrup from the warmer, and brought everything to the table.

One day at a time.

Well, that worked and all, except tomorrow might be the day. And if that was the case, we'd know our fate by sundown.

I only hoped it was the one we wanted.

CHAPTER TWELVE

DACIANA

THE MOUNTAIN OF BLANKETS on the floor beside the bed warmed my heart. It was a gift from my Alpha, his way of preparing for the nest he knew I would improve over the next few days of my cycle.

Night had fallen outside his windows, the full moon illuminating Andorra under a cascade of pale light.

Elias approached behind me, his arms circling my waist as we admired the evening together. "How are you feeling?" he asked softly.

I swallowed, knowing what he meant. "The cramps have started." A dull ache inside that typically elicited a deep-seated fear within me. Yet I felt oddly calm tonight, standing in the protection of my Alpha. For the first time ever, I had a male who could properly see me through my estrus.

Little butterflies took flight in my lower belly, excitement jittering up and down my spine.

Everything about this moment felt right. The way he held me, the heat pouring off his naked body into mine, and the hard promise growing against my backside.

Mmm, he would see to my every need. He already had, given the state of the bedroom. In addition to the variety of linens, he'd stocked up on water, snacks, and other useful tidbits to keep us happily cocooned in bliss together. For an Alpha who had never seen an Omega through her heat cycle, he was certainly doing an amazing job.

"Who helped you prepare?" I wondered out loud as I turned in his arms.

His midnight irises smiled down at me. "Jonas and Riley gave me some suggestions." He drew his thumb up my spine, his palm grasping the back of my neck while his opposite arm remained wrapped around my shoulder blades. "Now tell me how you're really feeling. Not just physically, but emotionally, too."

"I'm…" I trailed off, considering. "I'm at peace," I admitted softly. "Part of me is nervous, but I've never felt so secure. Usually I'm a ball of nerves at this point, shaking in the middle of the woods, praying no one finds me. Then the pain hits and I immediately regret my isolation, but it's so harsh that I can't do anything about it. And by the time I surface, I hate myself while knowing I'll repeat the entire process in less than a month. But not this time. With you… with you it's different."

He studied me for a long moment, his brows drawing downward. "I feel as if my entire life was meant to lead up to this moment," he marveled softly. "Like everything I've ever done has been for you, despite never knowing you existed until recently."

I licked my lips because I felt the same way. As if all the agony spent in the woods had been my way of saving myself for him—for my worthy mate. "I feel the same way."

Elias pressed his forehead to mine, his sigh feathering across my mouth. "I need to ask you something. Something difficult."

I frowned and pulled back to study him. "What is it?" I asked, my stomach twisting in a not-so-pleasant manner.

He cleared his throat, uncertainty scattering through his features.

Whatever he needed to ask wasn't going to be enjoyable.

And I suspected I knew exactly what he needed to know.

"Our fates will either be aligned or not by the end of your cycle," he began, confirming my suspicion on his topic of choice. "I need to know..." He cleared his throat once more. "I need to know how you want to proceed should we be unable to create life together."

My heart stopped beating, the very idea of us being incompatible causing my breath to freeze in my chest.

"We don't know anything yet," he rushed to add. "The reports Ceres provided all confirmed you're fertile and capable of procreating; we just don't know if you'll be able to accept my seed or not. And in the case you can't, I..." He sighed, his face falling. "I know how important procreation is to Omegas, Daciana. I would never want to take that away from you. Even if it means having to deny what I feel inside."

Wait... My forehead creased in confusion. "Feel inside?"

"That you're mine," he whispered. "Not claiming you has been one of the most difficult tasks I've ever faced, but I can't tie you to me without knowing if I can provide everything you need. It wouldn't be right. Yet, despite telling myself that repeatedly, my selfish need to claim you as mine continues to rise. So I need you to confirm your desires for me, out loud, to help keep that instinct at bay. Please."

"You haven't claimed me because you're worried about my ability to conceive your child," I translated.

He nodded. "And I know how much Omegas value children. I can't take that dream away from you."

"What about you?" I pressed, needing to ensure I understood. "Don't you want a child of your own?"

Elias turned inward, seeking the answer inside him, and sighed. "Yes, but I want you more. And I know that's selfish of me to admit. Which is why I need you to tell me your desires, so I can put your wants before my own."

"So if I'm unable to bear your offspring, you'd accept that." Not a question, but a statement. One underlined in shock. "You're an Alpha. Procreation is your ultimate achievement."

He chuckled. "Yeah, it's a desire, but finding the right mate is higher on my list. I suppose that makes me different from others, as you're right, most Alphas want an heir. While I would like one, it's not as important as securing a partner in life. Being an unmated Alpha is a lonely existence, Daciana. And after my experiences with you, well, Betas will never be enough anymore. Not when I know what it feels like to knot you."

I gaped at him. "How are we this deeply connected after so short a time together?" I whispered, awed. Because I felt the same way about him. While I longed for a child, I wanted him more. And something told me that wasn't a fleeting desire but one born of my very soul.

His gaze warmed, his lips curling softly at the sides.

"I don't know, sweetheart. But it's how I feel."

"It's how I feel, too." I went onto my toes to kiss him, my lips sealing over his as I poured all my emotions into the embrace.

This male surpassed all my expectations, proving himself worthier and worthier at every turn. And I wanted him to know how much I appreciated him, how I longed to be with him regardless of our biological differences.

If we couldn't have a baby, then we'd find another way to be together.

Andorra Sector was all about science, healthcare, and technology. If anyone could determine a path for us, it was the wolves residing under this dome.

I said as much out loud, earning me a soft growl from the Alpha gripping my neck. A fresh surge of need hit me between the thighs, my slick permeating the air as the beginning stage of my estrus began.

Whether he'd coerced it from me or fate had chosen that moment for my heat to start, I didn't know. Didn't care. Too lost in his mouth to ponder such frivolous details.

What mattered was that my soul had chosen him. My heart, too. And my body.

I encircled him with my arms, practically climbing upward to reach what I desired most—my center against his throbbing arousal.

"Yes," I hissed, my legs wrapping around his waist as he hoisted me into the air with one hand against my ass.

He seated himself inside me in a single thrust, the connection delicious and perfect.

My back hit the wall, his hips guiding our movements, his mouth a benediction against my own.

Oh, I loved this.

Him.

Our shared chemistry.

This beautiful moment.

Everything about our connection was perfect and right and one hundred percent mutual.

"Daciana," he breathed, his shaft owning me completely. I clamped down around him, urging him to pick up his pace, to drive deeper inside, to slam into that place I most desired.

And he did.

He gave everything to me.

His lips caressed mine. Traveled along my cheek. His teeth grazed my jaw.

"Yes, yes," I encouraged him, aware of his yearning, the bond he craved as much as I did. "Do it," I told him. "Make me yours."

The rest we could figure out later.

It was the *now* that I cared about most.

Our mating.

Our future.

Our lives blending together as one.

"Be sure," he said in a broken whisper. "Tell me you're sure."

"Bite me, Alpha," I demanded instead. "Claim me!"

"Fuck," he exhaled harshly, his groan one that rattled every ounce of my being. I vibrated against him, my ecstasy mounting.

"Now," I begged. "Please, Elias. Please now. While I still have my wits about me." Because once estrus took me under, I'd lose myself for hours. Would become a slave to the demands of my body and his, a screaming ball of pleasure and need that only my Alpha could satisfy.

But I had my mind now.

And I wanted to *remember* our joining.

"Please," I repeated, arching into him.

He cursed once more, his mouth skimming my pulse. "I can't... I need you too much." His teeth pierced my skin, the sharp sting jolting down my spine as a cloud of euphoria and rightness overwhelmed my insides, as a band encircled my heart.

A band inscribed with his name.

My soul melted to become one with his, our link taking hold and rooting deep inside us both.

Mine, my wolf hummed, the word falling from my lips in kind.

"Mine," Elias agreed, lapping at the blood trickling down my shoulder.

He kissed me, my essence thick in his mouth, as he fucked me with his tongue and his cock, driving me to the point of no return.

I screamed, my nails raking down his back, my sex pulsing in time with his arousal, as his knot latched on and forced me headfirst into the oblivion of my estrus.

Intense *need* overwhelmed me unlike any before. Even as I came, I desired more, his seed not enough to calm my inner beast.

My lips captured his, my teeth skimming his lip and biting down as agony ripped me in two. I needed him to fuck me harder. To take me within my nest. To pound me into another world of existence.

His hands were everywhere, his fingers exploring.

But it wasn't enough.

I cried.

Whined.

Pleaded for more.

Demanded his knot to return as soon as it disappeared.

Screaming at him to mount me.

I barely recognized myself, hardly understood that my hands were in the bedding now, my knees helping to balance me on all fours as he drove into me from behind.

"Yes, like that," I moaned, pressing into him for another harsh stroke.

His chest covered my back, his lips at my neck, his teeth in my skin as a delicious male growl reverberated down my spine.

I felt owned.

Possessed.

Utterly controlled.

And I adored it, craved more, needed him to grip me harder and fucking *thrust*.

Oh, he did exactly that, his hands hot clamps searing my hips as he introduced me to a whole new level of existence. One where I flew high and long and sighed on the way down.

Rapturous ripples cooled my violent hunger, allowing my mind to surface just long enough to note the way my mate held me protectively in his arms, his seed pouring inside me.

We were on our sides, my head pillowed against his arm, his damp torso curving around my back. *Spooning*, I thought dizzily. *We're spooning.*

Warmth spread through my veins, tickling my senses, my core awaking with renewed thirst.

He shushed me with a soothing rumble that quieted my instincts. I yawned, part of me noting the sun brightening the sky outside.

How long have we been fucking? I wondered idly.

My sore limbs and aching insides suggested it'd been hours. Maybe even days.

Mmm, but we weren't done. Just peaking in the midst of our frenzy.

I wanted to do more.

To taste him.

My fingers disappeared between my thighs, seeking

the juices of our shared arousal and bringing the decadent flavor to my lips. I moaned, arching into him.

"Fuck, you're insatiable," he accused with a husky laugh.

I whined in response, shifting backward into him in a needy manner that earned me a slap to my hip.

And more of that delicious purring.

I rolled against him, writhing, *needing*.

His lips traced a wet path up my neck, his teeth skimming the shell of my ear. "Tell me what you want, baby. Scream it for me."

"*Everything*," I panted. "Take me everywhere."

He slipped from my pussy, doing the exact opposite of what I declared. Then slid between the crease of my ass. "Here?" he asked, his breath hot against my throat.

Mmm, I knew this was coming. He'd been slowly warming me up with his fingers for hours, preparing me to take him. And while I preferred his knot, I also wanted to experience this. "Please," I said, pushing into him. "Fuck me."

"Fuck you where?" he asked, his hand dipping around to thrum my pulsating bundle of nerves. "Tell me how you want me to fuck you."

"My ass, Elias," I hissed. "I want to feel you everywhere. Always. Make me yours in all ways."

"You're already mine," he replied, entering me with a swift twist of his hips.

I cried out at the sudden fullness, so different from the other way he'd taken me, yet amazing, too. He continued to stroke my center, his thumb applying just the right amount of pressure to provide the friction I required.

"Elias," I whimpered, his intrusion taking me to another of those dark, forbidden places my body craved.

Harsh.

Violent.

Savage.

Thrusts.

I met each of them with an undying eagerness, my gratification looming and disappearing too quickly for me to grasp.

Tears blanketed my cheeks.

His touch driving me insane.

Until he pinched my clit, twisting it sharply and *forcing* the orgasm to mount and crest from my core. His name left my lips on a shriek, my throat hurting from all the sounds I'd forced through it during our time together. But I couldn't stop shouting, his groan of satisfaction music to my ears as he came deep inside my ass.

No knot.

Because it wasn't the right place.

Which meant he'd recover quickly and be able to take me again.

And again.

And again.

"My mouth," I told him, gulping in air. "You need to fuck my mouth."

"I will," he promised. "Just as soon as I make you come all over my cock again."

"Mmm," I murmured, pleased with that reply.

My hands went to the bedding surrounding us, my need to rearrange our pillowy heaven taking over. It had to be right for our next mating. The perfect position.

The fullness in my backside left as Elias rolled to his back. I climbed over him as his seed seeped from the crevice of my ass.

He'd need to take me there again, to ensure I was his in all ways.

I'd enjoy it.

Demand more.

Until I felt completely filled with his seed and satisfied that we were joined in every way.

His midnight gaze glistened up at me as my breasts brushed his chest, my palms plumping the pillow beneath his head. "Next, we will fuck like this," he declared. "With you riding me."

I committed to that plan with a gentle sound of contentment, then continued my job of securing our nest while he used a washcloth to remove some of the residual fluids from our bodies.

When his cock eventually stirred against his thigh, I took my cue and straddled him.

He groaned, the tendons of his neck stretching as he tossed his head back in the perfect display of hedonism. I made sure he was completely inside before leaning down to bite the strong muscle of his throat, longing to mark him in the same way he did me. He jolted in surprise but didn't stop my blunt teeth from entering his skin.

I sat back, satisfied with the way his blood painted my lips, and began to ride, just the way he wanted.

And all too soon, we were coming again in unison, the part of him I yearned for most clinging to my walls and spilling his essence into my womb.

On and on we fucked. We played. We memorized each other in every intimate manner possible. I swallowed his seed, loving the way his knot pulsed at the base of his shaft when I took him deep into my mouth. He came inside my ass again. We fucked with him on top. Me on top. Up against the headboard. Once with me hanging off the bed with my hands braced on the floor. With my legs in the air. Another time with my face buried in the bed, where he forced me to lick up our previous lovemaking while he fucked me from behind.

Every. Possible. Way.

He introduced me to a world of bliss unlike anything I could have anticipated.

Marked me as his.

Allowed me to claim him in kind.

Screamed.

Moaned.

And fucked ourselves into oblivion.

Until, finally, days later, my high began to subside and the aches in my muscles took over from endless harsh use.

If Elias felt similarly, he didn't show it. But he bore the scratches of my nails, the bite marks from my teeth, and the general redness of our bodies coming together in an explosion of savagery and violence.

I panted beneath him, my latest orgasm rolling off me in a wave of pleasure and pain.

"Mmm, there's my Daciana," he murmured, running his nose along my cheekbone. "My beautiful, definitely pregnant mate."

My heart stopped at his words.

Pregnant.

I palmed my belly, trying to focus, but the vestiges of ecstasy kept trying to pull me under, to keep me in the throes of estrus just a little longer.

"I can sense my seed inside you," he whispered, his lips caressing my ear. "We've created a life together, Daciana."

"You're sure?" I asked on an exhale, my chest burning from lack of air. I needed to breathe. But I couldn't. Not now. Not until I *knew*.

"Yes," he said, smiling against my mouth. "I'm certain."

Joy bubbled out of me, my lungs inflating on a sharp inhale, then left in a sound that was part laugh, part sob.

Our wolves are destined for each other, I thought, delirious with excitement. "We're mates."

"Yes, baby. We are," he agreed, capturing my lips in a kiss that branded every inch of my soul. "You're mine."

"And you're mine," I breathed, elation unlike anything I'd ever known warming me from head to toe. "My Elias."

"My Daciana."

I giggled. "I like the way that sounds."

"Me, too," he said softly, nuzzling my nose. "And I love the way it feels."

"Mmm, yeah," I agreed, sighing into him. "You know what else I love?"

"What?" His midnight gaze smiled down at me as he balanced himself on his elbows on either side of my head.

"You," I admitted. "I love you."

A breathtaking grin graced his features, stealing the air from my lungs all over again. "I love you, too, Daciana of Andorra Sector."

My lips parted, the correction lying on my tongue. Until I realized it didn't need to be corrected at all.

Because I was officially Daciana of Andorra Sector, just as he said.

Mate of Commander Elias.

Pregnant with his child.

An Ash Wolf Omega claimed by an X-Clan Wolf Alpha.

Immeasurable happiness burst from my chest as I wrapped my arms around him. "Make love to me, mate."

"After days of fucking, that's my mate's first request?" he asked, sounding amused. "Mmm, you really were made for me, weren't you?"

I arched my hips into his, my eyebrows lifting. "Now, Alpha."

"So demanding, my Omega," he mused, nibbling on

my chin. "Good thing I know how to meet your needs."

"Prove it," I dared.

"Oh, I intend to, baby." His lips drifted to my ear. "Now scream, Daciana. Tell the entire sector you're mine."

EPILOGUE

ELIAS

One Week Later

DACIANA SAT BESIDE ME AT THE COUNCIL TABLE, her hands clasped demurely in her lap. I reached over to grab one, giving it a gentle squeeze before brushing a kiss against her temple. "It's going to be all right, baby," I whispered.

She nodded, her lip caught between her teeth.

Ander sat on my other side, the screen before us black while we waited for the Shadowlands Sector Alpha to appear.

Presenting Daciana to the council had sucked, their questions intrusive. But she'd taken it all in stride, her breathing steady, her heart rate a calm beat to my ears.

Not even Enzo or Artur had fazed her.

Yet Dušan was another matter entirely.

When Ander had suggested Daciana remain for the call, she'd clammed up. I nearly took her from the room, but she'd assured me she could handle this. That she *needed* to be here.

And she was right.

For the deal to go through, Andorra Sector had to prove that we'd upheld our part of the bargain and kept Daciana safe.

Now that we knew Ash Wolves and X-Clan Wolves were indeed suited for one another, we needed this agreement to work.

The council had looked at Daciana with hunger in their eyes, their longing palpable. The very prospect that Ander might be able to supply them Omegas for mating had left them all but bowing down to their superior.

Well, almost all of them.

Artur and Enzo had their own opinions, which, fortunately, the majority didn't share. It was hard for the Alphas to deny the potential when presented with my new pregnant mate. Our early detection technology proved what my wolf already knew, for those who refused to rely on their senses. A simple sniff confirmed my mate was with child. Ceres just provided additional proof for those causing trouble in the back.

Dušan appeared with a tree over his shoulder, as per usual. He never took these calls from an office. I wasn't even sure he had one.

"Ander," he greeted.

"Dušan," my Sector Alpha replied. "We've completed our trials."

The Shadowlands Sector Alpha nodded, his light blue eyes shifting to Daciana. "You look well, little one. I hope that means they are treating you responsibly?"

"Better than the Alphas back home," she muttered under her breath.

Dušan arched a brow. "I'm sorry. I didn't catch that."

Oh, he totally caught it. He was just giving her a chance to adjust her attitude before addressing him again.

I squeezed her hand again, this time in gentle warning. Pissing off the male whom Ander wanted to negotiate with would not end well for any of us.

She cleared her throat and started again. "I chose Elias as my mate, and I am pregnant with his child."

Not exactly an answer to his question, but the Alpha seemed to accept it with a nod. "I assume the courting aspect of our agreement was upheld?"

This time her lips curled slightly, a hint of pink brushing her cheeks. "Yes, sir. Elias proved to be a most worthy mate."

I kissed her temple, silently thanking her for the kindness of her words. "Love you," I whispered in her ear.

"Love you, too," she mouthed back at me, her blue eyes sparkling as she met my gaze.

It took physical restraint not to pull her into my arms and devour her. As soon as this meeting ended, I could take her. And I would. Maybe even on the table, just so Enzo and Artur would have to smell it during our next meeting.

"I'd planned to request a private meeting with Daciana to confirm her unforced affections, but I can see that won't be necessary at all," Dušan mused, his focus on me. "She chose well."

"She did," I agreed. Because how couldn't I? She'd chosen me, and I wouldn't have it any other way. "But you're still welcome to question her privately, if she agrees to it."

"It's not needed," she said, her tone underlined in strength and intensity. "I chose him. He chose me. And we are mated. I believe the other Omegas will be treated fairly as well, so long as Ander is Alpha of Andorra Sector."

My best friend glanced at her with a brief look of surprise before focusing on Dušan. "I've managed this sector for nearly a century. I don't plan on stopping anytime soon."

"Let's hope not," the Ash Wolf Alpha replied. "You're the only X-Clan Wolf I've agreed to negotiate with."

Ander gave a nod. "Likewise." He cleared his throat. "Well, as you can see, our experiment was a success. We're ready to proceed with the rest of the transaction."

Nine more Omegas in exchange for a shit ton of advanced technology, including transportation and healthcare items.

We'd already supplied one colossal shipment in exchange for Daciana. Now we would multiply that export by nine, in exchange for the Ash Wolf Omegas.

It was the first step of many in our attempt to stabilize the hormonal imbalance present in Andorra Sector. If Ander succeeded, he'd secure his place at the top for at least another century, likely longer as wolves lived a very long time.

He just needed to get his own mating figured out because he reeked of dissatisfaction.

Whatever discord existed between him and Kat was definitely a problem. One I told him he needed to fix as soon as our call with Dušan had ended.

"I'm working on it" was all Ander said before stalking off in the direction of the elevators.

Daciana stood beside me, following the disgruntled Alpha with her gaze, her eyebrows pulling down. "He's not very happy for someone who just secured a shipment of Omegas."

"Because the Omega he wants isn't playing his game," I replied.

"Then perhaps he should change tactics," she suggested.

"Let's hope he does," I said, shaking my head. "But I doubt he will." Ander Cain was a stubborn-ass wolf. And so was his intended mate.

"Hmm, that's too bad. I like playing with you," Daciana murmured, her fingers trailing up my dress shirt as she pressed her body into mine. "In fact, I already have a game in mind."

I slid my arms around her waist, intrigued. "What did you have in mind, princess?"

One light blonde eyebrow lifted, a devious twinkle gracing her azure gaze. "I run. You chase."

"Oh, that's my favorite game," I admitted.

"Mine, too."

I pressed my lips to hers, giving her a taste of her future by sliding my tongue against hers. "I'll give you a five-minute head start," I whispered.

"From when we reach the bottom floor," she said, adding a clever stipulation to our rules.

I grinned. "All right."

She drew her teeth along my jaw, her expression alight with excitement. "Let's go."

I followed her into the elevator, kissing her the whole way down. Then watched hungrily as she stripped. I tossed my clothes onto the pile she'd created, not caring if we lost them in the building.

Then I stepped out onto the ground floor on bare feet as her fur coat brushed my thighs. "Run fast, Daciana," I told her softly, rolling my shoulders. "Your five minutes begins now."

She bolted for the doors, the security guards opening them for her with amused expressions.

And exactly five minutes later, I took off after her on four legs, my nose tracking the trail her sweet scent left behind.

Mine, my wolf growled, thrilled by my little mate's favorite game.

Because when I found her, I'd receive the biggest prize of all—*my mate.*

THE X-CLAN UNIVERSE CONTINUES WITH WINTER'S ARROW

True love is a myth.
A trick.
A way to subdue the heroine and take everything from her.

Winter Snow

My "true love" conspired with my stepmother to have me killed and stole my throne.

But they failed.

I've been in hiding and refining my vengeance. I'm no longer the damsel they mistook me for once upon a time. I'm coming for them. And my kingdom, too.

Who needs dwarves when you have wolves?
Who needs blades when you have arrows?

My name used to be Snow. Now they call me the Winter's Arrow. Because I'm here to destroy them all.

Kazek Flor

I'm not a prince but an Alpha. And I take what I want, when I want it. So when I found an Omega princess dying in the woods, I took her and made her mine.

I'll train her. Embolden her. Help her seek the vengeance she is owed. Then, together, we'll take down Winter Sector and the wicked Queen of Mirrors.

Run fast, little wolves.
Your former princess is about to rise with me by her side.
And we're thirsting for your blood.

Author's Note: This is a standalone Snow White retelling and based in the X-Clan Omegaverse universe.

WHERE THE X-CLAN SERIES BEGAN
ANDORRA SECTOR

Katriana Cardona

My life ended the moment the X-Clan found me.

Bitten.
Turned.
And claimed by *him*.

My genetic markers label me as a rare Omega. But inside, I'm all female alpha. And I will not heel. Not even to the Alpha of Andorra Sector.

Ander Cain promises me protection.
A new world of pleasure and pain.
But he wants all of me in return.
Even if it means taking me by force.

I'll be damned if I give up my inner fight. I spent the last twenty-one years battling the walking dead. These wolves won't know what hit them when I'm through.

Ander Cain

My life began the moment I found her, my darling little mate. She's the force of nature Andorra Sector needs to give us hope for a future. A reason to keep going and to protect our lands from the zombie infestation beyond.

Yet she refuses to play by our rules.

Born in a time where humans will do anything to survive, she's not used to the pack hierarchy or the laws our kind abides by. Oh, but she'll learn. And I'll thoroughly enjoy being the one to train her.

Katriana Cardona can fight me all she wants, but in the end, she will be mine. Whether she submits or not.

INTERESTED IN FINDING OUT WHAT HAPPENED TO DUŠAN AND HIS RUNAWAY OMEGA?

Check out *Shadowlands Sector* by Mila Young:

They call me an outcast, weak.

I've fought my whole life for survival, running from an attack on my family I ended up hiding with the Ash Wolves. This one move might be my biggest mistake of all. And I'm the queen of mistakes…

I let them believe I'm broken, let them believe the lies. I let them believe anything they want…as long as it isn't the truth.

There's a monster inside me, one made of teeth and claws and terrifying need. I swallow it down, hiding under the pretense of being normal. But I'm not normal. I'm anything but.

Bonding is the only thing that will save us—me and the Ash pack. Only I need someone strong enough to fight the darkness inside me…and savage enough to stay.

Will the three ruthless alphas help me…when they find out the truth of what I am?

This is a standalone shifter paranormal romance story for those who love alpha protectors, wolf shifters, and steamy scenes.

ACKNOWLEDGMENTS

Thank you, Matt, for all your love and support. You'll always be my number one.

This book wouldn't have been possible without my alpha/beta team: Katie, Allison, Jean, Tracey & Joy. Thank you all so much for reading and convincing me to publish this novella.

Bethany: Thank you for squeezing in the edits on this project. I appreciate you more than you know!

Louise & Diane: You both are my rocks. Thank you for giving me the freedom to hide and write. Without you, X-Clan: The Experiment wouldn't exist.

Chas & Kathy: Thank you for organizing my chaotic schedule of releases! You're both amazing.

And to the readers: Thank you for reading my very first novella. It was a lot of fun to write and I hope you enjoyed Daciana and Elias as much as I did.

Until next time… xx

ABOUT THE AUTHOR

USA Today Bestselling Author Lexi C. Foss loves to play in dark worlds, especially the ones that bite. She lives in Atlanta, Georgia with her husband and their furry children. When not writing, she's busy crossing items off her travel bucket list, or chasing eclipses around the globe. She's quirky, consumes way too much coffee, and loves to swim.

ALSO BY LEXI C. FOSS

Blood Alliance Series
Chastely Bitten
Royally Bitten
Regally Bitten

Dark Provenance Series
Daughter of Death
Son of Chaos

Immortal Curse Series
Blood Laws
Forbidden Bonds
Blood Heart
Elder Bonds
Blood Bonds
Angel Bonds
Blood Seeker

Mershano Empire Series
The Prince's Game
The Charmer's Gambit
The Rebel's Redemption

Midnight Fae Academy
Ella's Masquerade
Book One

X-Clan Series
Andorra Sector
The Experiment
Winter's Arrow